LITURGICAL ABUSE

A Cancer in the Church

LITURGICAL ABUSE

A Cancer in the Church

Edited by

Paul A. Mihalik , OCDS, M.Ed.
Lt.Col. USAF (Ret.)

Queenship

PUBLISHING COMPANY
P.O. Box 220 • Goleta, CA 93116
(800) 647-9882 • (805) 692-0043 • Fax: (805) 967-5133

About The Author

Mr. Mihalik is a retired Lt. Colonel of the United States Air Force; married to Lucy for 52 years. They have seven children and are members of the Secular Order of Discalced Carmelites. He taught as adjunct professor for ten years with Embry-Riddle Aeronautical University in Tucson, Arizona and has three Masters degrees in marriage counseling and education. He has spoken at various public appearances and Marian conferences.

Mr. Mihalik has authored the following published books:

The Final Warning, Queenship Pub.
The Virgin Mary, Fr. Gobbi, and the Year 2000, Queenship Pub.
The Nature of Angels, Queenship Pub.
Offering Of Suffering, Queenship Pub.

Mr. Mihalik's e-mail address is raphael@dakotacom.net
His phone number is 520-394-2018

Library of Congress Number # 2002141050

Published by:
    Queenship Publishing
    P.O. Box 220
    Goleta, CA 93116
    (800) 647-9882 • (805) 692-0043 • Fax: (805) 967-5133
    http://www.queenship.org

Printed in the United States of America

ISBN: 1-57918-180-5

Table of Contents

Introduction

INTRODUCTION

It required two re-writings of this introduction before I could adjust my initial feelings of inner turmoil resulting from the liturgical abuses that are seen today in so many Catholic Churches. Remembering that we must always try to keep our peace and realizing that anger leads to more anger and poor results I will attempt to provide some objective and clear assistance to those who are also disenchanted with some of the goings-on in the Church today.

The best course of action perhaps is to defend our Faith and its traditions and teachings with the attitude of a people seeking the truth and basing all our actions on the fruitful grounds of love, understanding, and compassion.

An acquaintance of mine in San Antonio, Texas informed me of the battle waged in his parish over the relocating of the tabernacle to a chapel outside of the church. Although he wrote to Rome and was supported by the Vatican in his belief, the priest has still apparently refused to comply with the Canon Law. Speakers address the religious education staff using four letter words while distorting traditional Catholic beliefs; a dissident ex-priest circumvents the Bishop's refusal to permit him to speak at a Church function, eventually speaking to church staff anyway; the Call To Action people influence key personnel in the Religious Education Centers of various dioceses; an Archdiocese has knowingly allowed members of Call To Action to TEACH THE RELIGIOUS EDUCATION TEACHERS; and the director of worship for an archdiocese promotes liturgical modernism.

Call To Action (CTA) is a national organization founded in 1976, made up of 18,000 members, and is hell-bent to promote women's ordination, creation spirituality, married priesthood, liturgical reform, select their own bishop, and even the Pope. They are effective in using small faith communities to approach with their ideas and use the groups in the communities to further their agenda. It is wise for all to be on the alert for the make-up and the agenda of Call To Action within their parishes.

This book will not answer every question concerning abuses in the liturgy. An attempt is made here to address those abuses that are the most commonly observed but seemingly never satisfactorily explained by the perpetrators. I leaned quite heavily on a number of sources to obtain the most professional and accurate answers and explanations possible that would go into a rather limited-size book.

Every now and then one comes across what we would call a gold-mine because of the richness, depth, and quality of the information discovered. As a new member of the amazingly resourceful organization called Catholics United For The Faith (CUF), I found an especially rich goldmine in my search for authentically documented liturgical abuses.

The purpose of the existence of CUF is to provide guidance and answers to the Catholic population concerning the many questions raised by the laity and some clergy because of the variance of "procedures" among the various parishes, and deviation from Canonically approved rubrics. I do not believe we can attribute these abuses to Vatican Council II. Rather, the interpretation by theologians, some bishops, and many priests seem to be more clearly the reason for some abuses. The spread and rapidity with which these abuses have taken place might even raise the question as to how frequent are these abuses due to wilful disobedience.

There are a few bishops in the Church today who are becoming more and more popular with the laity because of their staying within the bounds of tradition and the Magisterial teachings on faith and morals. There are some bishops who seem to be unaware of the liturgical shenanigans going on within their parishes

I have received permission from The Catholic World Report Magazine to reprint verbatim an outstanding article by Michael Rose, Editor of the St. Catherine *Review* and author of *The Renovation Manipulation*. In the February 2001 issue of The Catholic World Report, he confronts the belief that the Church is suffering from a shortage of priests because of a lack of vocations. In Chapter Three you will find his contention, based on numerous interviews with priests, that there is a deliberate effort to restrict the entrance of orthodox and Marian applicants into many of our seminaries, thus culling out the loyal candidates and admitting a predominance of the modernist and liberal minded. My suspicion is that it is these liberal-minded priests, now active in the Church, that are in most part responsible for the many liturgical abuses, and, in some cases, with the blessings of their bishops who refuse to do anything about it. Now is the time for much prayer and sacrifice by loyal believers—that these conditions will change quickly for the good of the Church.

Another resource which is offering outstanding service to the Catholic public is the St. Joseph Foundation. This organization offers free assistance to Catholics who suffer injustices and abuse in their parish or diocese. This is truly an invaluable Catholic service and they cannot be applauded too much for their courageous purpose and desire to serve the Church. They have helped hundreds of Catholics in need of legal guidance. No value can be placed on the benefit to the morale and peace of those who have been assisted. Catholics United For The Faith and the St. Joseph Foundation are sustained by contributions from the faithful, and are nonprofit organizations.

A lay group in San Antonio publishes a newsletter called The Defender and they are called Defenders of the Magisterium. Their address is P.O. Box 100492, San Antonio, Texas, 78201.

Contact the St. Joseph Foundation for assistance in using the Church's legal system to register complaints for injustices or liturgical abuse, etc.: 11107 Wurzbach Rd. Suite 601B, San Antonio, TX. 78230-2553. Ph: 210-697-0717; Fax: 210-699-9439.

One may write to Catholics United For The Faith for the protocol guide which explains in detail how to register legitimate complaints about liturgical abuses. Their address is: 827 North Fourth St. Steubenville, Ohio, 43952. Ph. is (740) 283-2484. Fax is (740) 283-4011. Web site: www.cuf.org

It is my hope that this little book will serve as a help to those who want to properly register objections or questions concerning liturgical abuses. Above all, it is hoped that some consolation is afforded the reader who desires to do the right thing as a loyal Roman Catholic by coming to the realization that the loyal Catholic has now been called to carry a very specially designed cross which can be offered for the salvation of souls and a strengthening of the one true Church.

Dedication

This book is dedicated to St.Therese of the Child Jesus and of the Holy Face, and St. Teresa of Avila, both Doctors of the Church and both of whom loved the Church more than themselves. May they intercede for our Catholic Church in this time of great tribulation and loss of faith.

Chapter One

Crisis In the Church

The experts seem to agree that anything can be "proven" by a manipulation of statistics gathered in the various polls. There is always some basic truth in the raw material of such polls and the statistics currently reflect that the percentage of Catholics that go on a regular basis to Confession is only about 3 percent. Less than 50% go to Sunday Mass regularly, and over 70% do not believe in the Real Presence in the Holy Eucharist. In Europe the figures are just as bleak, especially in the so-called Catholic countries of France and Italy where Church attendance on Sundays is about 3 percent. Spain fares just a little better.

Monsignor George Kelly, in his book *Battle For The American Church Revisited* (Ignatius Press), reveals a guerilla-type warfare going on inside the American Church and that the warfare by the American Catholic Church is fighting to change the Church's mission, its nature and the gospel. Monsignor Kelly describes in detail the struggle between Rome and the National Conference of Catholic Bishops and between Magisterial officers and religious superiors, theologians, and educators. Chaos reigns, the Church suffers in her people, and Christ weeps in His Heaven. More bishops must awaken to this great emergency; they must look to the example of the first Apostles of the Church, and emulate their courage and steadfastness, see their sense of duty and loyalty to the teaching of Jesus. We need to pray that they will live up to their prime responsibility to teach and preserve the true Faith which has been entrusted to them.

It is a serious matter to point the finger for this problem to some of the very shepherds charged with preserving the teachings of the church, but it cannot be denied that since the completion of Vatican Council II, conditions in the Church have gone downhill at a rapid pace—a pace that is almost impossible to explain unless some diabolical entity is behind this sad picture. The Holy Spirit was as involved with Vatican II as He was in all the previous councils. Pope John Paul II has repeatedly spoken of his love and respect for the work of the Council. Then what is the problem that could lead to the weakening of this great Catholic Faith? The experts again say it is the wrongful interpretation of Vatican II by the Modernists and liberals and their implementation of their erroneous version of the Council work within their dioceses.

A general loss of a sense of sin permeates our entire society, and the pathetic attendance at the Sacrament of Reconciliation opposed by the overwhelming attendance at the Sacrament of the Eucharist on Sundays and holy days is good evidence of this phenomenon among Catholics. It is heartbreaking when one must point the finger at the clergy as the cause of the problems in the Church. It is certainly recognized that there are hundreds and hundreds of dedicated priests and bishops, brothers and nuns who are loyal to the Magisterial teachings of the Church and who give totally of themselves to their people and the Church.

Confusion Among the Laity

There is confusion as to when children should be confirmed; when they should make their First Communion; whether they should make their First Confession before their First Communion; whether to kneel or stand at the consecration at Mass; whether to take Communion in the hand or on the tongue. There are very serious controversies in many dioceses concerning the trend toward a "modern" and, in the opinion of thousands, an ugly barn-like and sterile architecture which is void of the beauty and warmth which had been traditional in our Catholic churches. The complaint today is that it is just one more example of the Protestantizing of our faith which has grown out of the misguided understanding of some who have completely missed the boat and the intent behind the ecumenical movement.

Contempt Towards the Holy Father

The Faith is being watered-down in new interpretations by the theologians on the contents of the Bible and the longstanding teachings of the Church. Look at the deplorable reception Pope Paul VI received for his encyclical, Humanae Vitae. In her book, *Why Humanae Vitae Was Right*, author Janet E. Smith includes 21 essays by well-respected thinkers who provide the evidence that Pope Paul VI was not only right but he was also prophetic in his predictions of what would come in a runaway sensual world. And the bishops, with few exceptions, remain silent.

Disobedience of the Clergy

The liberals and theologians have been downright disobedient in not following the Vatican's guidelines on the administration and staffing of Catholic Colleges and Universities. Priests and nuns have actively participated on the college campuses in the pro-choice demonstrations. The Holy Father desires that members of the teaching staffs conform with the teachings of the Church or be removed from teaching positions. Some of the worst damage to the Catholic minds of University students has taken place, not in secular schools and campuses but in the theology departments of supposedly Catholic Universities. Some of our Irish friends and alumni of one of our most prominent and beloved Catholic Universities would not believe what has been taught and presented as Catholic theology. The Pope has recently put his foot down on the requirement for the Catholic Universities to comply—or else the removal of the recalcitrants will take place. Who would have ever thought that a pope would have to take such drastic action and make such threats to obtain compliance with his directives which have been promulgated for the good of the faithful?

In spite of the Holy Father's claim that we are in a new springtime of the Church, we are still faced with a condition in our seminaries and dioceses that simply must be overcome and quickly. Willful disobedience by those responsible for the teaching and preservation of our Faith is at least partly to blame for the unbelievably chaotic conditions in the Church globally. If even a few of our seminaries are producing the modernistic and liberal minded priests who no longer can relate to the traditional teachings of the Church, what can we expect will take place in the average parish in this country? It has already taken place; two generations of Catholics who know little or nothing about their Faith and are unable to share it with their own children. The very core of Catholic belief, the Real Presence in the Eucharist, is no longer a matter of belief among

70 percent or more Catholics.

Loss of the Sense of Sin

A loss of belief in the Real Presence can be attributed partially to the attitude toward sin—that almost anything goes now-a-days so who needs confession? But the answer is even more basic than that. In a discussion recently by two theologians on Mother Angelica's T.V. program it was stated that the very basic reason the disbelief in the Real Presence has grown so wildly is because of the very inadequate religious education programs in the dioceses. And now we ask the question—who is responsible for the inadequacy of these programs? It IS NOT only the Director of Religious Education. This person is hired by the parish priest and implements the goals of the program as outlined and specified by that priest. If that priest is one of our many modernists or liberals you can predict what the outcome of that program will be in every area of Catholic traditions and teachings. This weakness in our Catholic Education system will take years to overcome and rectify and there is no sign that anything is being done about it. There is apparently no agenda to face this serious problem by the Catholic Council of Bishops; at least it hasn't been made public so the average Catholic parishioner knows anything about such plans for their children.

Error, Evil, and Incompetence in Seminaries Cause A False Shortage of Priests

You might be wondering why the cause of poor religious education has been laid primarily on the liberal clergy. In Chapter Four you will find the results of a study by Mr. Michael Rose, who was identified in the Introduction of this book. His revelations, which were obtained from interviewing hundreds of priests, speak of the deplorable tactics exercised in some dioceses to screen out any seminary applicant who proves on interview that he is loyal to the Virgin Mary and follows the orthodox track of Faith.

Many of the Church's problems, including liturgical abuses, can be attributed, in part, to poor seminary training. Another probable factor is a willful disobedience against the Magisterial teaching of the Church by the Modernists and liberals who want desperately to create the American Catholic Church, divorced from Rome.

Two Bishops Curtail Perpetual Adoration
of The Eucharist

With regards to the Eucharist, some of you might remember the days of the Forty Hours Devotion during which the exposition of the Eucharist was held in Churches all over America. People regularly attended that devotion which had them in adoration before the Monstrance which contained the body, blood, soul, and divinity of Our Lord. In the year 2000 the bishop of one of our southern dioceses ordered his parishes to stop all Perpetual Adoration of the Holy Eucharist. He authorized a maximum of two days only in any one year for the Perpetual Adoration of the Eucharist. His reasoning was that Perpetual Adoration detracted from the Mass.

One can only wonder about the motivation behind such an action when his people preferred to adore the Eucharist even at great inconvenience to themselves in following the schedule around the clock. I have a copy of his letter to all of his parish priests. No priest that I have spoken to or have written to on Catholic television has been able to follow the reasoning offered. I sit here now trying to imagine how one can justify depriving his people of the graces that come to them and the entire Church from the sacrificial acts that necessarily accompany the devotion of Perpetual Adoration.

Some see this as a sign of the forces at work to eventually deny the presence of Christ in the Eucharist. One priest theologian said on television that "I know of no other dioceses except for Los Angeles and St. Petersburg Florida, that forbid or curb the frequency of Adoration Chapels nor of Eucharistic Holy hours... I have never seen any notice from Rome and the Holy Father but a constant encouragement in favor of Eucharistic Adoration, and indeed, to Perpetual Eucharistic Chapels too. I know that not only will such practice not detract from the Mass but it will actually greatly increase our love and devotion for the Liturgy."

Rights of The Laity To Object to Abuses and Injustices

Following are two amazing documents from solid Catholic priests who are considered staunch supporters of the traditional orthodox Roman Catholic Faith. They capsulize the current scary conditions within the Church viewed by loyal priests and from the standpoint of the loyal Catholic laity:

A Prophetic Warning
By Father John A. Hardon, S.J.

I believe the breakdown of religious life in the Western world is a phenomenon that is unique in the history of Christianity. There have been, since the last half of this century, more departures from Catholicism, more closing of Catholic churches, more dioceses that have been secularized than ever before in the history of Christianity. We are living in the most deeply de-Catholicized age of Christianity.

The United States has been one of the main victims. In general we may say the more academically educated, the more wealthy and the richer in this world's goods a nation was, the greater has been the departure from Jesus Christ. Only God knows what the future will be, but judging by the last five hundred years, there has been a far-reaching breakdown of authentic Christianity. It began, of course, with the rise of Protestantism, originated by a Catholic priest and a member of a religious order.

In the Catholic Church we have seen the most widespread breakdown of the priesthood and authentic consecrated life. In my thirty-third year of working for the Holy See—just a few things I can share with you. The Holy See seriously wonders how much of the Catholic Church will survive in wealthy prosperous nations of the Western world like our own. What then is the remedy? There is only one way which the revolution can be reversed—and it had better be reversed. Professed Catholics who call themselves Christians must reexamine their faith. We must be sure we believe that God became man in the Person of Jesus Christ. We must believe that when God became man He instituted the Holy Eucharist. We must believe that the consecrated life—of consecrated poverty, consecrated chastity, constant obedience is most pleasing to Jesus Christ. When God became man He made sure He lived a life, I repeat, of consecrated chastity, obedience and poverty. What I want to share with you is that, not only religious life, but the Catholic Church will be preserved only where there are, hear it, Catholics who are living martyrs. Do you hear me?

Ordinary Catholics will not survive this revolution. They must be Catholics who are thoroughly convinced that God became Man in the person of Jesus. They must be convinced there is only one supreme authority on earth: the authority of Jesus Christ vested in the Vicar of Christ. What the Church needs, desperately needs, is strong believing Catholics. Otherwise, one nation after another, like our own, will be wiped out as a Christian country.

Lord Jesus, we beg you, strengthen our faith in Your divinity, even our conviction that You are God Who became Man to live a consecrated life to teach us what authentic honest-to-God Catholicism is all about. Protect us, Dear Lord, from the widespread mania which has penetrated countries like ours. It is not coincidental we have lost most of the religious in the United States. Dear Lord, how we need a deep faith, the faith of martyrs today, because only those who are convinced that to live a consecrated life means to live a martyr's life. Dear Lord, we are not together here unless we believe You, Jesus, are our God. But help us, we beg You, to become more and more like You; living examples of what the early Church showed the pagan world: that you are our God and we are Your creatures, born in this world to convert a pagan world to Christianity. (From a presentation at the 1999 National Meeting of the Institute on Religious Life. There were present— Cardinal George, Bishops Bruskewitz, Doran, and Tomlin; many Mother Superiors, and Father Superiors.)

Darkness

Those of us who love the Church, grieve over the Church. If you know what's been happening over these several years now, you grieve over the Church. For there is darkness that has entered even inside the very sanctuary of God. It is a fact that immoral theology has been taught in certain seminaries and Catholic universities for many years. I said immoral theology not moral theology in universities, colleges, catholic high schools, it's a travesty. Things that have long been held to be mortal sins objectively taken, are called to be normal human behavior.., artificial contraception, sexual relations outside of marriage, masturbation, you name it. Now all of a sudden, moral theology has changed in its essence. Darkness, doctrinal errors, someone may have told you that Jesus isn't really present in the Eucharist, it's a sign, a mere symbol.

It is the Lord, it is the lord. The emphasis has shifted from the lord to the people. The people are important, we are the body of Christ, but I tell you this, you won't be the Body of Christ unless you receive the Body of Christ and He's more important than we are. For he is the head of His Mystical Body. Unless you have lost your head, realize that Jesus is the one who is in charge of His Church. The teaching on the Blessed Mother has gone from light to darkness. When I was a boy we didn't hear theologians dare suggest that there might be an error in the teaching of the virgin birth, the immaculate conception, the assumption of Our lady into Heaven and if you asked the average Catholic if She was the Mediatrix of all grace, no eyebrow would raise of course.

The teaching concerning the Holy Father (was not questioned). All Catholics loved the Holy Father, they would not question his teachings. We hadn't gained that much arrogance. But now, many think nothing criticizing, attacking and condemning the teachings of the successor of St. Peter... darkness.

Sometimes we feel like we are in a cocoon. The liturgy, we wonder sometimes, what happened. Oh, many good things happened the last thirty years, but some not so good. It was good to throw open the windows to allow the fresh air, especially the breath of God, to come in. To open the church to the world to give the world the benefit of the Church's teaching. But as one Cardinal

Archbishop said at the council, "Be very careful that you do not cross a line, for yes it is good that we be open to the world... the world is good... meaning the world as creation, the world as the theater of redemption. Indeed set us to be open to the world and give the world everything we have to offer. But do not confuse that with the world as a spirit. The spirit of the world is something else. And if that foul wind comes into the open windows, look out." The bishop of Buse, Belgium made that intervention at the Second Vatican Council. It was prophetic.

And so we look at some of these things and wonder what's going on. Sometimes we feel alienated, discouraged, even despondent. Indeed, the darkness closes in. We are in that dark place with Jesus, we have to remember that. He suffered and died. He was buried in the tomb. The darkness closes around His Mystical Body, and we are tempted at times to lose heart. The devil's great weapon is discouragement. I see it everywhere. I have experienced it myself. The evil one wants to discourage us, he would have us believe perhaps that our Church is all gone, it is falling apart. That we will never have a celebration of the Eucharist with the kind of reverence that we used to of course.

But we can and do have reverence in the contemporary celebration of the Eucharist. But in many places we have problems. And so we have to be strengthened. We have to strengthen each other. We have to remember that yes, there is a passion, yes, there is a death, yes, there is a going down into the darkness of the tomb. We find ourselves there now.

But there is a resurrection, the dawn is coming, this is Holy Saturday and the Lord is about to rise. Just as surely as the sun rises every morning, the Son of Justice, the Son of God, The Son of Mary, the Son of Man rises on the third day. Remember very well when the darkness closes in. When the temptation to become cynical, discouraged, despondent closes in on you, remember though evil has its hour, the hour of the Lord is near at hand. We have to trust the Lord. The world and the Church belong to God. God is in charge of the world and the Church.

Don't be an ostrich who buries his head in the sand, but acknowledge the reality that we have problems, big time. We had better not deny that and when we deny that we facilitate evil. All that evil requires is that good men remain silent. And we don't want to be guilty of that kind of silence which enables and facilitates evil.

*Taken from a Holy Saturday talk given
by Fr. John Corapi, S.O.LT., 1998*

WORDS OF WISDOM
From The Breviary to the Guardians of the Faith:

Watch yourself and watch your teaching. Persevere at tasks. By doing so you will bring to salvation yourself and all that hear you. *1 Timothy* 4:16

Remember your leaders who spoke the word of God to you; consider how their lives ended, and imitate their faith. Jesus Christ is the same yesterday, today, and forever. Do not be carried away by kinds of strange teachings. *Hebrews* 13:7-9a

To the elders among you I, a fellow elder, a witness of Christ's sufferings and sharer in the glory that is to be revealed, make this appeal. God's flock is in your midst; give it a shepherd's care. Watch over it willingly as God would have you do, not under constraint, and not for shameful profit either, but generously. Be examples to the flock, not lording it over those assigned to you, so that when the Chief Shepherd appears, you will win, for yourselves the unfading crown of glory. *1 Peter* 5:1-4

If we cannot turn to the shepherds of the flocks in trust and faith, then what will become of the Church? What will it take before sufficient spiritual leaders of our Church begin to attack the problems with a real sense of urgency?

It is not gainful to exaggerate the situation today in the Church concerning worship of the Eucharistic mystery. To illustrate that the Vatican itself recognizes the serious problem involving liturgical abuses there follows immediately the document issued by the Sacred Congregation for the Sacraments and Divine Worship on April 3, 1980. The document is titled *Instruction on Certain Norms Concerning the Worship of the Eucharistic Mystery.* It seems today that this document has been largely put aside and ignored by many to whom it was directed. Some changes have been issued since this document was first presented; for example, women altar severs are now permitted, but the abuses addressed concerning the Eucharist are still a serious problem.

Chapter Two

Inaestimabile Donum—Instruction on Certain Norms Concerning the Worship of the Eucharistic Mystery

Issued by the Sacred Congregation for
Divine Worship and the Sacraments, April 3, 1980

Following the letter that Pope John Paul II addressed on 24 February 1980 to the Bishops and, through them, to the Priests, and in which he again considered the priceless gift of the Holy Eucharist, the Sacred Congregation for the Sacraments and Divine Worship is calling to the Bishops' attention certain norms concerning worship of this great mystery.

These indications are not a summary of everything already stated by the Holy See in the documents concerning the Eucharist promulgated since the Second Vatican Council and still in force, particularly in the Missale Romanum, [1] the Ritual De sacra Communione et de cultu Mysterii eucharistici extra Missam, [2] and the Instructions Eucharisticum Mysterium, [3] Memoriale Domini, [4] Immensae Caritatis, [5] and Liturgicae Instaurationes. [6]

This Sacred Congregation notes with great joy the many positive results of the liturgical reform: a more active and conscious participation by the faithful in the liturgical mysteries, doctrinal and catechetical enrichment through the use of the vernacular and the wealth of readings from the Bible, a growth in the community sense of liturgical life, and successful efforts to close the gap between life and worship, between liturgical piety and personal piety, and between liturgy and popular piety.

But these encouraging and positive aspects cannot suppress concern at the varied and frequent abuses being reported from different parts of the Catholic world: the confusion of roles, especially regarding the priestly ministry and the role of the laity (indiscriminate shared recitation of the Eucharistic Prayer, homilies given by lay people, lay people distributing communion while the priests refrain from doing so); an increasing loss of the sense of the sacred (abandonment of liturgical vestments, the Eucharist celebrated outside church without real need, lack of reverence and respect for the Blessed Sacrament, etc.); misunderstanding of the ecclesial character of the liturgy (the use of private texts, the proliferation of unapproved Eucharistic Prayers, the manipulation of the liturgical texts for social and political ends). In these cases we are face to face with a real falsification of the Catholic liturgy: "One who offers worship to God on the Church's behalf in a way contrary to that which is laid down by the Church with God-given authority and which is customary in the Church is guilty of falsification." [7]

None of these things can bring good results. The consequences are—and cannot fail to be—the impairing of the unity of faith and worship in the Church, doctrinal uncertainty, scandal and bewilderment among the People of God, and the near inevitability of violent reactions.

The faithful have a right to a true Liturgy, which means the Liturgy desired and laid down by the Church, which has in fact indicated where adaptations may be made as called for by pastoral requirements in different places, or by different groups of people. Undue experimentation, changes and creativity bewilder the faithful. The use of unauthorized texts means a loss of the necessary connection between the lex orandi and the lex credendi. The Second Vatican Council's admonition in this regard must be remembered: "No person, even if he be a priest, may add, remove or change anything in the liturgy on his own authority." [8] And Paul VI of venerable memory stated that: "Anyone who takes advantage of the reform to indulge in arbitrary experiments is wasting energy and offending the ecclesial sense." [9]

A. The Mass

1. "The two parts which in a sense go to make up the Mass, namely the liturgy of the word and the Eucharistic liturgy, are so closely connected that they form but one single act of worship." [10] A person should not approach the table of the bread of the Lord without having first been at the table of his word. [11] Sacred Scripture is therefore of the highest importance in the celebration of Mass. Consequently there can be no disregarding what the Church has laid down in order to ensure that "in sacred celebrations there should

be a more ample, more varied and more suitable reading from sacred scripture." [12] The norms laid down in the Lectionary concerning the number of readings, and the directives given for special occasions are to be observed. It would be a serious abuse to replace the word of God with the word of man, no matter who the author may be. [13]

2. The reading of the Gospel passage is reserved to the ordained minister, namely the deacon or the priest. When possible, the other readings should be entrusted to a reader who has been instituted as such or to other spiritually and technically trained lay people. The first reading is followed by a responsorial psalm, which is an integral part of the liturgy of the word. [14]

3. The purpose of the homily is to explain to the faithful the word of God proclaimed in the readings, and to apply its message to the present. Accordingly the homily is to be given by the priest or the deacon. [15]

4. It is reserved to the priest, by virtue of his ordination, to proclaim the Eucharistic Prayer, which of its nature is the high point of the whole celebration. It is therefore an abuse to have some parts of the Eucharistic Prayer said by the deacon, by lower minister, or by the faithful. [16] On the other hand the assembly does not remain passive and inert: it unites itself to the priest in faith and silence and shows its concurrence by the various interventions provided for in the course of the Eucharistic Prayer: the responses to the Preface dialogue, the Sanctus, the acclamation after the consecration, and the final Amen after the Per Ipsum. The Per Ipsum itself is reserved to the priest. This Amen especially should be emphasized by being sung, since it is the most important in the whole Mass.

5. Only the Eucharistic Prayers included in the Roman Missal or those that the Apostolic See has by law admitted, in the manner and within the limits laid down by the Holy See, are to be used. To modify the Eucharistic Prayers approved by the Church or to adopt others privately composed is a most serious abuse.

6. It should be remembered that the Eucharistic Prayer must not be overlaid with other prayers or songs. [17] When proclaiming the Eucharistic Prayer, the priest is to pronounce the text clearly, so as to make it easy for the faithful to understand it, and so as to foster the formation of a true assembly entirely intent upon the celebration of the Memorial of the Lord.

7. Concelebration, which has been restored in the Western Liturgy, manifests in an exceptional manner the unity of the priesthood. Concelebrants must therefore pay careful attention to the signs that indicate that unity. For example, they are to wear the prescribed vestments, they are to occupy the place appropriate to their ministry as concelebrants, and they are to observe faithfully the other norms for the seemly performance of the rite. [18]

8. Matter of the Eucharist. Faithful to Christ's example, the Church has constantly used bread and wine mixed with water to celebrate the Lord's Supper. The bread for the celebration of the Eucharist, in accordance with the tradition of the whole Church, must be made solely of wheat, and, in accordance with the tradition proper to the Latin Church, it must be unleavened. By reason of the sign, the matter of the Eucharist celebration "should appear as actual food." This is to be understood as linked to the consistency of the bread, and not to its form, which remains the traditional one. No other ingredients are to be added to the wheaten flour and water. The preparation of the bread requires attentive care, to ensure that the product does not detract from the dignity due to the Eucharistic bread, can be broken in a dignified way, does not give rise to excessive fragments, and does not offend the sensibilities of the faithful when they eat it. The wine for the Eucharistic celebration must be of "the fruit of the vine" (Lk 22:18) and be natural and genuine, that is to say not mixed with other substances. [19]

9. Eucharistic Communion. Communion is a gift of the Lord, given to the faithful through the minister appointed for the purpose. It is not permitted that the faithful should themselves pick up the consecrated bread and the sacred chalice; still less that they should hand them from one to another.

10. The faithful, whether religious or lay, who are authorized as extraordinary ministers of the Eucharist can distribute Communion only when there is no priest, deacon or acolyte, when the priest is impeded by illness or advanced age, or when the number of the faithful going to communion is so large as to make the celebration of Mass excessively long. [20] Accordingly, a reprehensible attitude is shown by those priests who, though present at the celebration, refrain from distributing Communion and leave this task to the laity.

11. The Church has always required from the faithful respect and reverence for the Eucharist at the moment of receiving it.

With regard to the manner of going to Communion, the faithful can receive it either kneeling or standing, in accordance with the norms laid down by the Episcopal Conference. "When the faithful communicate kneeling, no other sign of reverence towards the Blessed Sacrament is required, since kneeling is itself a sign of adoration. When they receive Communion standing, it is strongly recommended that, coming up in procession, they should make a sign of reverence before receiving the Sacrament. This should be done at the right time and place, so that the order of people going to and from Communion is not disrupted." [21]

The Amen said by the faithful when receiving Communion is an act of personal faith in the presence of Christ.

12. With regard to Communion under both kinds, the norms laid down by the Church must be observed, both by reason of the reverence due to the Sacrament and for the good of those receiving the Eucharist, in accordance with variations in circumstances, times and places. [22]

Episcopal Conferences and Ordinaries also are not to go beyond what is laid down in the present discipline: the granting of permission for Communion under both kinds is not to be indiscriminate, and the celebrations in question are to be clearly defined, well disciplined, and homogeneous. [23]

13. Even after Communion the Lord remains present under the species. Accordingly, when Communion has been distributed, the

sacred particles remaining are to be consumed or taken by the competent minister to the place where the Eucharist is reserved.

14. On the other hand, the consecrated wine is to be consumed immediately after Communion and may not be kept. Care must be taken to consecrate only the amount of wine needed for Communion.

15. The rules laid down for the purification of the chalice and the other sacred vessels that have contained the Eucharistic species must be observed. [24]

16. Particular respect and care are due to the sacred vessels, both the chalice and paten for the celebration of the Eucharist, and the ciboria for the Communion of the faithful. The form of the vessels must be appropriate for the liturgical use for which they are meant. The material must be noble, durable and in every case adapted to sacred use. In this sphere judgment belongs to the Episcopal Conference of the individual regions.

Use is not to be made of simple baskets or other receptacles meant for ordinary use outside the sacred celebrations, nor are the sacred vessels to be of poor quality or lacking any artistic style.

Before being used, chalices and patens must be blessed by the Bishop or by a priest. [25]

17. The faithful are to be recommended not to omit to make a proper thanksgiving after Communion. They may do this during the celebration, with a period of silence, with a hymn, psalm or other song of praise, [26] or also after the celebration, if possible by staying behind to pray for a suitable time.

18. There are of course various roles that women can perform in the liturgical assembly: these include reading the word of God and proclaiming the intentions of the prayer of the faithful. Women are not however permitted to act as altar servers. [27]

19. Particular vigilance and special care are recommended with regard to Masses transmitted by the audiovisual media. Given their

very wide diffusion, their celebration must be of exemplary quality. [28] In the case of celebrations that are held in private houses, the norms of the Instruction Actio Pastoralis of 15 May 1969 are to be observed. [29]

B. Eucharistic Worship Outside Mass

20. Public and private devotion to the Holy Eucharist outside Mass also is highly recommended: for the presence of Christ, who is adored by the faithful in the Sacrament, derives from the Sacrifice and is directed towards sacramental and spiritual Communion.

21. When Eucharistic devotions are arranged, account should be taken of the liturgical season, so that they harmonize with the liturgy, draw inspiration from it in some way and lead the Christian people towards it. [30]

22. With regard to exposition of the Holy Eucharist, either prolonged or brief, and with regard to processions of the Blessed Sacrament, Eucharistic Congresses, and the whole ordering of Eucharistic piety, the pastoral indications and directives given in the Roman Ritual are to be observed. [31]

23. It must not be forgotten that "before the blessing with the Sacrament an appropriate time should be devoted to readings of the word of God, to songs and prayers and to some silent prayer." [32] At the end of the adoration a hymn is sung and a prayer chosen from among the many contained in the Roman Ritual is recited or sung. [33]

24. The tabernacle in which the Eucharist is kept can be located on an altar, or away from it, in a spot in the church which is very prominent, truly noble and duly decorated, or in a chapel suitable for private prayer and for adoration by the faithful. [34]

25. The tabernacle should be solid, unbreakable, and not transparent. [35] The presence of the Eucharist is to be indicated by a tabernacle veil or by some other suitable means laid down by the competent authority, and a lamp must perpetually burn before it, as a

sign of honor paid to the Lord. [36]

26. The venerable practice of genuflecting before the Blessed Sacrament,whether enclosed in the tabernacle or publicly exposed, as a sign of adoration, is to be maintained. [37] This act requires that it be performed in a recollected way. In order that the heart may bow before God in profound reverence, the genuflection must be neither hurried nor careless.

27. If anything has been introduced that is at variance with these indications it is to be corrected.

Most of the difficulties encountered in putting into practice the reform of the liturgy and especially the reform of the Mass stem from the fact that neither priests nor faithful have perhaps been sufficiently aware of the theological and spiritual reasons for which the changes have been made, in accordance with the principles laid down by the Council.

Priests must acquire an ever deeper understanding of the authentic way of looking at the Church, [38] of which the celebration of the liturgy and especially of the Mass is the living expression. Without an adequate biblical training, priests will not be able to present to the faithful the meaning of the liturgy as an enactment, in signs, of the history of salvation. Knowledge of the history of the liturgy will likewise contribute to an understanding of the changes which have been introduced, and introduced not for the sake of novelty but as a revival and adaptation of authentic and genuine tradition.

The liturgy also requires great balance, for, as the Constitution Sacrosanctum Concilium says, it "is thus the outstanding means by which the faithful can express in their lives, and manifest to others, the mystery of Christ, and the real nature of the true Church. It is of the essence of the Church that she be both human and divine, visible and yet invisibly endowed, eager to act and yet devoted to contemplation, present in this world and yet not at home in it. She is all these things in such a way that in her the human is directed and subordinated to the divine, the visible likewise to the invisible, action to contemplation, and this present world to that city yet to come, which we seek." [39] Without this balance, the true face of Christian liturgy becomes obscured.

In order to reach these ideals more easily it will be necessary to foster liturgical formation in seminaries and faculties [40] and to facilitate the participation of priests in courses, meetings, assemblies or liturgical weeks, in which study and reflection should be properly contemplated by model celebrations. In this way priests will be able to devote themselves to more effective pastoral action, to liturgical catechesis of the faithful, to practical training, to training animators of the assembly, to enriching progressively the repertoire of songs, in a word to all the initiatives favoring an ever deeper understanding of the liturgy.

In the implementation of the liturgical reform great responsibility falls upon national and diocesan Liturgical Commissions and Liturgical Institutes and Centers, especially in the work of translating the liturgical books and training the clergy and faithful in the spirit of the reform desired by the Council.

The work of these bodies must be at the service of the ecclesiastical authority, which should be able to count upon their faithful collaboration. Such collaboration must be faithful to the Church's norms and directives, and free of arbitrary initiatives and particular ways of acting that could compromise the fruits of the liturgical renewal.

This Document will come into the hands of God's ministers in the first decade of the life of the Missale Romanum promulgated by Pope Paul VI following the prescriptions of the Second Vatican Council.

It seems fitting to recall a remark made by that Pope concerning fidelity to the norms governing celebration: "It is a very serious thing when division is introduced precisely where congregavit nos in unum Christi amor, in the Liturgy and the Eucharistic Sacrifice, by the refusing of obedience to the norms laid down in the liturgical sphere. It is in the name of Tradition that we ask all our sons and daughters, all the Catholic communities to celebrate with dignity and fervor the renewed liturgy." [41] The Bishops, "whose function it is to control, foster and safeguard the entire liturgical life of the Church entrusted to them," [42] will not fail to discover the most suitable means for ensuring a careful and firm application of these norms, for the glory of God and the good of the Church.

Endnotes

1. Ed. typica altera, Romae 1975.
2. Ed. typica, Romae 1973.
3. Sacred Congregation of Rites, 25 May 1967: Acta Apostolicae Sedis (AAS) 59 (1967), pp. 539–573.
4. Sacred Congregation for Divine Worship, 29 May 1969: AAS 61 (1969), pp. 541–545.
5. Sacred Congregation for the Discipline of the Sacraments, 29 January 1973: AAS 65 (1973), pp.264–271.
6. Sacred Congregation for Divine Worship, 5 September 1970: AAS 62 (1970), pp. 692–704.
7. St. Thomas, Summa Theologiae, 2-2, q. 93, a.1.
8. Second Vatican Council, Sacrosanctum Concilium, 22, 3.
9. Paul VI, Address of 22 August 1973: L'Osservatore Romano, 23 August 1973.
10. Second Vatican Council, Sacrosanctum Concilium, 56.
11. Cf. ibid., 56; cf. also Second Vatican Council, Dei Verbum, 21.
12. Second Vatican Council, Sacrosanctum Concilium, 35.
13. Cf. Sacred Congregation for Divine Worship, Instruction Liturgicae Instaurationes, 2, a.
14. Cf. Institutio generalis Missalis Romani, 36.
15. Cf. Sacred Congregation for Divine Worship, Instruction Liturgicae Instaurationes, 2, a.
16. Cf. Sacred Congregation for Divine Worship, Circular Letter Eucharistiae Participationem, 27 April 1973: AAS 65 (1973), pp. 340–347, 8; Instruction Liturgicae Instaurationes, 4.
17. Cf. Institutio generalis Missalis Romani, 12.
18. Cf. ibid., 156, 161–163.
19. Cf. ibid., 281–284; Sacred Congregation for Divine Worship, Instruction Liturgicae Instaurationes, 5; Notitiae 6 (1970), 37.
20. Cf. Sacred Congregation for the Discipline of the Sacraments, Instruction Immensae Caritatis, 1.
21. Sacred Congregation of Rites, Instruction Eucharisticum Mysterium, 34. Cf. Institutio generalis Missalis Romani, 244 c, 246 b, 247 b.
22. Cf. Institutio generalis Missalis Romani, 241–242.
23. Cf. ibid., end of 242.
24. Cf. ibid., 238.
25. Cf. Institutio generalis Missalis Romani, nos. 288, 289, 292, 295; Sacred Congregation for Divine Worship, Instruction Liturgicae Instaurationes, 8; Pontificale Romanum, Ordo Dedicationis Ecclesiae et Altaris, p. 125, no. 3.
26. Cf. Institutio generalis Missalis Romani, 56 j.
27. Cf. Sacred Congregation for Divine Worship, Instruction Liturgicae Instaurationes, 7.
28. Cf. Second Vatican Council, Sacrosanctum Concilium, 20; Pontifical Commission for Social Communications, Instruction Communio et Progressio, 23 May 1971: AAS 63 (1971), pp. 593–656, no. 151.
29. AAS 61 (1969), pp. 806–811.

30. Cf. Rituale Romanum, De sacra Communione et de cultu Mysterii eucharistici extra Missam, 79–80.
31. Cf. ibid., 82-112.
32. Ibid., 89.
33. Cf. ibid., 97.
34. Cf. Institutio generalis Missalis Romani, 276.
35. Cf. Rituale Romanum, De sacra Communione et de cultu Mysterii eucharistici extra Missam, 10.
36. Cf. Sacred Congregation of Rites, Instruction Eucharisticum mysterium, 57.
37. Cf. Rituale Romanum, De sacra Communione et de cultu Mysterii eucharistici extra Missam, 84.
38. Cf. Second Vatican Council, Lumen Gentium.
39. Second Vatican Council, Sacrosanctum Concilium, 2.
40. Cf. Sacred Congregation for Catholic Education, Instruction on Liturgical Formation in Seminaries In ecclesiasticam futurorum sacerdotum formationem, 3 June 1979.
41. Consistorial Address of 24 May 1976: AAS 68 (1976), p. 374.
42. Second Vatican Council, Decree Christus Dominus, 15.

This document taken from:

The Catholic Liturgical Library http://www.catholicliturgy.com

Chapter Two
Part B

Specific Abuses and Appropriate Church Directives

Chapter Two provided the entire text of Inaestimabile Donum as a reference for the reader. It outlined the overall condition in the Church concerning the liturgical abuses concerning the Sacraments and the Liturgy of the Mass, which had come to the attention of the Vatican.

In this part of Chapter Two a very informative document is provided for your convenience. Specific liturgical abuses are addressed by the author, Ms. Clementine Lenta, who received approval from the Roman curia to distribute this document to the Faithful. Excerpts from Inaestimabile Donum are cited as the answer and correction to specific liturgical abuses that, because of their frequent occurrences in the liturgy, demanded special attention in such a document. Ms. Lenta decided to publish this information as an assist to those of us who have seen such abuses in the administration of some of the sacraments. Her publication is titled *Liturgical Directives* and addresses abuses concerning the Sacraments of the Eucharist and Reconciliation, and the Mass itself. Ms. Lenta cites the official directive of the Church which speaks to the individual abuses. One of these directives is Inaestimabile Donum, which was written by the Sacred Congregation for the Sacraments and Divine Worship in 1980 and approved by Pope Paul II to stem the tide of liturgical abuses. Another directive referred to is Dominacae Cenae (1980), and finally referral is made to Canon Law for certain abuses. The Code of Canon Law as it pertains to the Eucharist is also contained in this book for the convenience of the reader (see Chapter Seven of the present book).

Ms. Lenta's document *Liturgical Directives* now follows:

Liturgical Directives

The Holy Sacrifice of the Mass:
    Is it celebrated properly and reverently in your parish?
The Sacrament of Reconciliation (Confession):

Is it administered properly and reverently in your parish?

The Sacrament of the Holy Eucharist (Holy Communion): Is it administered and received properly and reverently in your parish?

The Holy Sacrifice of the Mass

On April 3, 1980 the Sacred Congregation for the Sacraments and Divine Worship issued Inaestimabile Donum (Instruction on Certain Norms Concerning Worship of the Eucharistic Mystery). It was approved by Pope John Paul II on April 17, 1980 and was addressed to all the Catholic Bishops of the world. Its purpose is to prevent abuses and allay confusion. As its Introduction states:

"None of these things can bring good results. The consequences are—and cannot fail to be—the impairing of the unity of faith and worship in the Church, doctrinal uncertainty, scandal, and bewilderment among the People of God, and the near inevitability of violent reactions.

"The faithful have a right to a true liturgy, which means the liturgy desired and laid down by the Church . . . Undue experimentation, changes and creativity bewilder the faithful . . . The Second Vatican Council's admonition in this regard must be remembered: 'No person, even if he be a priest, may add, remove or change anything in the liturgy on his own authority'."

Since many people are indeed confused regarding certain practices associated with the Eucharist, here are a number of official statements issued and approved by the Apostolic See through *Inaestimabile Donum, Dominicae Cenae, the Canon Law Code (1983)* and other documents:

Adding to or Changing Liturgical Texts

Inaestimabile Donum (1980)—Item No. 5 states:
"To modify the Eucharistic Prayers approved by the

Church or to adopt others privately composed is a most serious abuse."

Non-Scriptural Readings During the Liturgy

Inaestimabile Donum—Item No. 1 states:
"It would be a serious abuse to replace the Word of God with the word of man, no matter who the author may be."

Congregation Joining in the Eucharistic Prayer
"Through Him, with Him, in Him, etc."

Inaestimabile Donum—Item No. 4 states:
"It is reserved to the priest, by virtue of his ordination, to proclaim the Eucharistic Prayer. It is therefore an abuse to have some parts of the Eucharistic Prayer said by the deacon, by a lower minister or by the faithful."

Homily Given by a Religious Sister, Brother or Lay Person

Inaestimabile Donum—Items. No. 2 and No. 3 state:
"The reading of the Gospel passage is reserved to the ordained minister, namely the priest or deacon . . . The purpose of the homily is to explain to the faithful the Word of God proclaimed in the Readings and to apply its message to the present. Accordingly, the homily is to be given by the priest or the deacon."

Priest's Genuflections

The Roman Missal—Revised by Decree of the Second Vatican Ecumenical Council (1970)—Item No. 233 states:
"Three genuflections are made during Mass: after the elevation of the host, after the elevation of the chalice, and before communion.

"If there is a tabernacle with the blessed sacrament in the sanctuary, a genuflection is made before and after Mass and whenever passing in front of the sacrament."

Altar Girl Servers

Inaestimabile Donum—Item No. 18 states:
"There are various roles that women can perform in the liturgical assembly including reading the Word of God and proclaiming the intentions of the Prayer of the Faithful. However, women are not permitted to act as altar servers."

Use of Altar Breads or Wine

Inaestimabile Donum—Item No. 8 states:
"The bread of the celebration of the Eucharist, in accordance with the tradition of the whole Church, must be made solely of wheat, and, in accordance with the tradition proper to the Latin Church, it must be unleavened . . . No other ingredients are to be added to the wheat flour and water . . . The wine for the Eucharistic Celebration must be of the fruit of the vine and be natural and genuine, that is to say, not mixed with the other substances."

The Liturgy and Dancing

Notitiae (Instructions for Sacraments and Divine Worship) Vol. XI, (1975) pp. 202-205 state:
"Dance has never constituted an essential part in the official liturgy of the Latin Church. If local Churches have introduced the dance, at times even in the temples, this was on occasion of feasts in order to show feelings of jubilation and devotion. But the dance always took place outside the liturgical actions. Conciliar decisions have often condemned the religious dance, as not befitting worship, and also because it could degenerate into disorders . . .

hence, it is not possible to introduce something of that sort in the liturgical celebration; it would mean bringing into the liturgy one of the most desacralized and desacralizing elements: and this would mean the same as introducing an atmosphere of profanity, which would easily suggest to those present worldly places and profane situations."

Place for the Celebration of the Holy Sacrifice

Canon Law (1983)—Item No. 932 (1) states:
"The celebration of the Eucharist is to be performed in a sacred place, unless in a particular case necessity demands otherwise; in such a case the celebration must be done in a respectable place."

Liturgical Vestments

Canon Law (1983)—Item No. 929 states:
"In celebrating and administering the Eucharist, priests and deacons are to wear the liturgical vestments prescribed by the rubrics."

The Blessed Sacrament

Adoration of the Blessed Sacrament

Inaestimabile Donum—Item No. 20 states:
"Public and private devotion to the Holy Eucharist outside Mass also is highly recommended; for the presence of Christ, who is adored by the faithful in the sacrament, derives from the sacrifice and is directed towards sacramental and spiritual Communion."

Inaestimabile Donum—Item No. 22 states:
"With regard to exposition of the Holy Eucharist, either prolonged or brief, and with regard to processions of the Blessed Sacrament, eucharistic congresses, and the

whole ordering of eucharistic piety, the pastoral indications and directives given in the Roman Ritual are to be observed."

Canon Law (1983)—Item No. 942 states:

"It is recommended that in these same churches and oratories an annual solemn, exposition of the Most Holy Sacrament be held during a suitable period of time, even if not continuous, so that the local community may meditate and may adore the Eucharistic Mystery more profoundly, but this kind of exposition is to be held only if a suitable gathering of the faithful is foreseen and the established norms are observed."

Dominicae Cenae (1980)—Item No. 3 states:

"Adoration of Christ in this sacrament of love must also find expression in various forms of Eucharistic devotion: personal prayer before the Blessed Sacrament, hours of adoration, periods of exposition—short, prolonged, and annual (Forty Hours) — Eucharistic benediction, Eucharistic processions, Eucharistic congresses. A particular mention should be made at this point of the Solemnity of the Body and Blood of Christ as an act of public worship rendered to Christ present in the Eucharist (Feast of Corpus Christi) . . . All this corresponds to the general principles and particular norms already long in existence but newly formulated during or after the Second Vatican Council.

"The encouragement and the deepening of Eucharistic worship are proofs of that authentic renewal which the Council set itself as an aim and of which they are the central point . . . The Church and the world have a great need of Eucharistic worship. Jesus waits for us in this sacrament of love. Let us be generous with our time in going to meet Him in adoration and in contemplation that is full of faith and ready to make reparation for the great faults and crimes of the world. May our adoration never cease."

Genuflecting Before the Blessed Sacrament

Inaestimabile Donum—Item No. 26 states:
   "The venerable practice of genuflecting before the Blessed Sacrament, whether enclosed in the tabernacle or publicly exposed, as a sign of adoration, is to be maintained."

The Tabernacle in Which the Eucharist is Kept

Inaestimabile Donum—Items No. 24 and No. 25 state:
   "The tabernacle in which the Eucharist is kept can be located on an altar, or away from it, in a spot in the Church which is very prominent, truly noble and duly decorated, or in a chapel suitable for private prayer and for adoration by the faithful.
   "The tabernacle should be solid, unbreakable, and not transparent. The presence of the Eucharist is to be indicated by a tabernacle veil or by some other suitable means laid down by the competent authority, and a lamp must perpetually burn before it, as a sign of honor paid to the Lord."

Respect and Care Due to the Sacred Vessels

Inaestimabile Donum—Item No. 16 states:
   "Particular respect and care are due to the sacred vessels, both the chalice and paten for the celebration of the Eucharist and the ciboria for the Communion of the faithful. The form of the vessels must be appropriate for the liturgical use for which they are meant. The material must be noble, durable, and in every case adapted to sacred use. . .
   "Use is not to be made of simple baskets or other recipients meant for ordinary use outside the sacred celebrations, nor are the sacred vessels to be of poor quality or lacking any artistic style."

The Sacraments

In His great and loving mercy, God has given us seven special gifts—the Seven Sacraments. These sacraments, if properly used, are gifts of inestimable value in aiding us in our journey towards God. Unfortunately, they are not always appreciated, not always received as God intended and His Church directs. Sometimes they are even abused. Among these are the Sacrament of Reconciliation (Confession) and the Sacrament of Holy Eucharist (Holy Communion).

The Sacrament of Reconciliation (Confession)

The Necessity and Benefit

The Rite of Penance (Revised Roman Ritual, 1973)—Items No. 7A- 7B state:

"To obtain the saving remedy of the Sacrament of Penance, according to the plan of our merciful God, the faithful must confess to a priest each and every grave sin which they remember upon examination of their conscience.

"Frequent and careful celebration of this sacrament is also very useful as a remedy for venial sins. This is not a mere ritual repetition or psychological exercise but a serious striving to perfect the grace of Baptism so that, as we bear in our body the death of Jesus Christ, His life may be seen in us ever more clearly. In Confession of this kind, penitents who accuse themselves of venial faults should try to conform more closely to Christ, and to follow the voice of the Spirit more attentively."

General Confession and Absolution

The Rite of Penance—Items No. 31-34 state:

"Individual, integral confession and absolution remain the only ordinary way for the faithful to reconcile themselves with God and the Church, unless physical or moral impossibility excuses from this kind of Confession.

"Particular, occasional circumstances may render it lawful and even necessary to give general absolution to a number of penitents without their previous individual confession.

"In addition to cases involving danger of death, it is lawful to give sacramental absolution to several of the faithful at the same time, after they have made only a generic confession but have been suitably called to repentance, if there is grave need . . . This may happen especially in mission territory but in other places as well and also in groups of persons when the need is established.

"General absolution is not lawful, when confessors are available, for the sole reason of the large number of penitents, as may be on the occasion of some major feast or pilgrimage.

"The judgment and the decision concerning the lawfulness of giving general sacramental absolution are reserved to the Bishop of the diocese, who is to consult with the other members of the episcopal conference.

"In order that the faithful may profit from sacramental absolution given to several persons at the same time, it is absolutely necessary that they be properly disposed. Each one should be sorry for his sins and resolve to avoid committing them again. He should intend to repair any scandal and harm he may have caused and likewise resolve to confess in due time each one of the grave sins which he cannot confess at present. These dispositions and conditions, which are required for the validity of the sacrament, should be carefully recalled to the faithful by priests.

"Those who receive pardon for grave sins by a common absolution should go to individual Confession before they receive this kind of absolution again, unless they are impeded by a just reason. They are strictly bound, unless this is morally impossible, to go to Confession within a year. The precept which obliges each of the faithful to confess at least once a year to a priest all the grave sins which he has not individually confessed before also remains in force in this case too."

Place of Confession

Canon Law (1983)—Item No. 964 states:
"No. 1. The proper place to hear sacramental confessions is church or an oratory."

"No. 2. The conference of bishops is to issue norms concerning the confessional, seeing to it that confessionals with a fixed grille between penitent and confessor are always located in an open area so that the faithful who wish to make use of them may do so freely."

"No. 3. Confessions are not to be heard outside the confessional without a just cause."

The Sacrament of the Holy Eucharist (Holy Communion)

Proper Disposition For Receiving Holy Communion

Dominicae Cenae—Item No. 7 states:
". . . We must always take care that this great meeting with Christ in the Eucharist does not become a mere habit, and that we do not receive Him unworthily, that is to say, in a state of mortal sin."

Dominicae Cenae—Item No. 11 states:
". . . Sometimes, indeed quite frequently, everybody participating in the Eucharistic assembly goes to Communion; and on some such occasions, as experienced pastors confirm, there has not been due care to approach the Sacrament of Penance so as to purify one's conscience. This can of course mean that those approaching the Lord's table

find nothing on their conscience, according to the objective law of God, to keep them from this sublime and joyful act of being sacramentally united with Christ. But there can also be, at least at times, another idea behind this; the idea of the Mass as only a banquet in which one shares by receiving the Body of Christ in order to manifest, above all else, fraternal communion. It is not hard to add to these reasons a certain human respect and mere 'conformity'."

Daily Communion

Canon Law (1983)—Item No. 917 states.

"A person who has received the Most Holy Eucharist may receive it again on the same day only during the celebration of the Eucharist in which the person participates. . ." (Except in case of danger of death).

Use of Extraordinary Lay Ministers

Inaestimabile Donum—Item No. 10 states:

"The faithful, whether Religious or lay, who are authorized as extraordinary ministers of the Eucharist can distribute Communion only when there is no priest, deacon or acolyte, when the priest is impeded by illness or advanced age, or when the number of the faithful going to Communion is so large as to make the celebration of Mass excessively long. Accordingly, a reprehensible attitude is shown by those priests who, though present at the celebration, refrain from distributing Communion and leave this task to the faithful."

Lay People Picking Up Consecrated Hosts and/or Handing Them to One Another
and
Lay People Taking the Chalice from the Altar or Table and/or Handing it to One Another

Inaestimabile Donum—Item No. 9 states:

"Eucharistic Communion is a gift of the Lord given to the faithful through the minister appointed for this purpose. It is not permitted that the faithful should themselves pick up the consecrated Host and the sacred Chalice; still less that they should hand them from one to another."

Holy Communion Under Both Species

Inaestimabile Donum—Item No. 12 states:

"With regard to Communion under both kinds, the norms laid down by the Church must be observed, both by reason of the reverence due to the sacrament and for the good of those receiving the Eucharist, in accordance with variations in circumstances, times, and places.

"Episcopal conferences and ordinaries also are not to go beyond what is laid down in the present discipline: the granting of permission for Communion under both kinds is not to be indiscriminate, and the celebrations in question are to be specified precisely . . .

Method of Receiving Holy Communion

Dominicae Cenae—Item No. 11 states:

"In some countries the practice of receiving Communion in the hand has been introduced. This practice has been requested by individual episcopal conferences and has received approval from the Apostolic See. However, cases of a deplorable lack of respect toward the Eucharistic Species have been reported, cases which are imputable not only to the individuals guilty of such behavior but also to the pastors of the church who have not been vigilant enough regarding the attitude of the faithful toward the Eucharist. It also happens, on occasion, that the free choice of those who prefer to continue the practice of receiving the Eucharist on the tongue is not taken into account in those places where the distribution of Communion in the hand has been authorized . . ."

Instruction of the Congregation for Divine Worship, Memoriale Domini (1969)—Item No. 1 states:
"The new method of administering Communion should not be imposed in a way that would exclude the traditional usage."

Posture in Receiving Holy Communion

Inaestimabile Donum-- Item No. 11 states:
"The Church has always required from the faithful respect and reverence for the Eucharist at the moment of receiving It.

"With regard to the manner of going to Communion, the faithful can receive it either kneeling or standing, in accordance with the norms laid down by the episcopal conference . . ."

Thanksgiving After Communion

Inaestimabile Donum—Item No. 17 states:
"The faithful are to be recommended not to omit to make a proper thanksgiving after Communion. They may do this during the celebration, with a period of silence, with a hymn, psalm, or other song of praise or also after the celebration, if possible, by staying behind to pray for a suitable time."

Children's Communion Before Confession

Quam Singulari 1 Acta Apostolicae Sedis: this decree issued on August 8, 1910 by (Saint) Pope Pius X declared:
"The right time for beginning to receive the Sacraments of Penance and Holy Eucharist is judged to be the age which, in Church documents, is called that of reason or discretion. This age, both for Confession and for Communion, is the point where the child begins to think, i.e., around seven years, more or less. From this time on he bears the obligation to satisfy the two commandments of Confession and Communion . . . The custom of not admitting children to Confession or of never giving them absolution, although they have reached the age of reason, is certainly to be rejected . . . It is expedient that the custom of putting Confession before First Communion should be preserved."

Addendum of the General Catechetical Directory
This document issued on April 11, 1971 by the Religious Instruction Committee of the Sacred Congregation for the Clergy and approved by Pope Paul VI reaffirms this decree.

Sanctus Pontifex
This official document was issued on May 24, 1973 by the Sacred Congregation for the Discipline of the Sacraments and the Sacred Congregation for the Clergy, approved by Pope Paul VI, and signed by their respective prefects, Antonio Cardinal Samore and John Cardinal Wright. It strengthens these directives. The declaration stated that First Confession must precede the reception of First Communion. It also stated that all experiments regarding First Communion before First Confession must be halted by the end of the 1972-1973 scholastic year.

Canon Law (1983)—Item No. 914 states:

"It is the responsibility, in the first place of parents and those who take the place of parents as well as of the pastor to see that children who have reached the use of reason are correctly prepared and are nourished by the divine food as early as possible, preceded by sacramental confession . . ."

Holy Communion Administered to Non-Catholics

Canon Law (1983)—Item No. 844 (4) states:

"If the danger of death is present or other grave necessity, in the judgment of the diocesan bishop or the conference of bishops, Catholic ministers may licitly administer these sacraments to other Christians who do not have full communion with the Catholic Church, who cannot approach a minister of their own community and on their own ask for it provided they manifest Catholic faith in these sacraments and are properly disposed."

(It is evident from this Canon Law that the indiscriminate distribution of Holy Communion to Non-Catholic Christians is not permitted.)

The Role of the Hierarchy, the Clergy and the Laity

Hierarchy

Inaestimabile Donum—Conclusion:

"The bishops, whose function it is to control, foster, and safeguard the entire liturgical life of the Church entrusted to them, will not fail to discover the most suitable means for ensuring a careful and firm application of these norms, for the glory of God and the good of the Church."

Clergy

Dominicae Cenae—Item No. 12 states:

". . . The priest as minister, as celebrant, as the one who presides over the Eucharistic assembly of the faithful, should have a special sense of the common good of the Church, which he represents through his ministry, but to which he must also be subordinate, according to a correct discipline of faith. He cannot consider himself a 'proprietor' who can make free use of the liturgical text and of the sacred rite as if it were his own property, in such a way as to stamp it with his own arbitrary personal style . . ."

Laity

Among the documents of Vatican II is the *Decree on the Apostolate of the Laity* which clearly defines the role and responsibility of the laity in the Church. The Council's *Dogmatic Constitution on the Church* (items No. 33–No. 38) also states pertinent information concerning the role of the laity. For example, item No. 37 declares (in part), "The laity have the right, as do all Christians, to receive in abundance from their sacred pastors the spiritual goods of the Church especially the assistance of the Word of God and the Sacraments . . . (he) is permitted and sometimes even obliged to express his opinion on things which concern the good of the Church. . ."

The importance and the responsibility of the role of the laity was emphasized by Cardinal Luigi Ciappi, personal theologian of Popes Pius XII, John XXIII, Paul VI, John Paul I and John Paul II. In a dialogue with reporters, Farley Clinton and Christopher De Sales, published in the *National Catholic Register*, September 26, 1982, concerning some of the repudiated or abandoned fundamental aspects of the Catholic Faith, the Cardinal stated: "The faithful have a right to appeal to their pastors, their bishops and also the apostolic delegate to express their difficulties in these areas. If that doesn't work, they can write to the Holy See, to the competent authorities. They can also write to the Holy Father directly. Vatican II made it clear that the faithful have a duty to collaborate in assuring the truths of the Catholic Faith."

It is indeed apparent that there are abuses and neglect in the celebration of the Holy Sacrifice of the Mass and the administration and reception of the Sacraments, particularly regarding the Sacrament of Reconciliation and the Sacrament of the Holy Eucharist.

It is significant that Pope John Paul II, Christ's Vicar on earth, not only issued *Dominicae Cenae* and *Inaestimabile Donum*—both of which contain directives relating to the Holy Sacrifice of the Mass, Holy Communion and Adoration Or the Blessed Sacrament—but that he also chose *"Reconciliation and Penance in the Mission of the Church"* as the topic of the 1983 Synod.

It is also noteworthy that the Holy Father has emphasized his concern about liturgical abuses and the need for correction in such statements as the following:

"As you well know, the theory according to which the Eucharist forgives mortal sin, without the sinner having recourse to the sacrament of Penance, is not reconcilable with the teaching of the Church. It is true that the sacrifice of the Mass, from which all grace comes to the Church, obtains for the sinner the gift of conversion, without which forgiveness is not possible, but that does not at all mean that those who have committed a mortal sin can approach Eucharistic Communion without having first become reconciled with God by means of the priestly ministry."

Pope John Paul II—December 4, 1981

(From an address to the Italian Bishops of the Episcopal Conference of Abruzzi and Molise on their "ad limina apostolorum" visit on December 4, 1981. Published in the English edition of *L'Osservatore Romano,* January 18,1982 issue.)

"It is necessary to recognize the existence of a certain crisis in the Sacrament of Penance. Many people no longer see in what way they have sinned, and even less, have possibly sinned seriously; nor, above all, why they should ask forgiveness before a representative of the Church; others give as an excuse that confessions were too tainted with routine and formalism, etc. There are, besides, serious reasons for astonishment and anxiety when one sees, in certain areas, so many of the faithful receiving the Eucharist when such a small number of them has recourse to the Sacrament of Reconciliation. On this point, good catechesis should lead the faithful to preserve the consciousness of their state of sinfulness and to understand the necessity and sense of a personal process of reconciliation before receiving, with the Eucharist, all its fruits of renewal and unity with Christ and his Church.

"The objection is sometimes made that priests, taken up with other tasks and often few in number, are not available for this kind of ministry. Let them remember the example of the saintly Cure d'Ars and so many other pastors who, even in our own day, thanks be to God, practice what has been called 'the asceticism of the confessional.' For we are all at the service of the members of the people of God entrusted to our zeal and, I would say, of each of them . . ."

(From an address to a group of French Bishops of the Eastern Ecclesiastical Region "ad limina apostalorum" visit, April 2, 1982. Published in the English edition of *L'Osservatore Romano,* August 16-23, 1982 issue.)

Forgiveness for Abuses

Pope John Paul II concluded *Dominicae Cenae (Item No. 12)* by stating: "... I would like to ask forgiveness—in my own name and in the name of all of you, venerable and dear brothers in the Episcopate—for everything which, for whatever reason, through whatever human weakness, impatience or negligence, and also through at times partial, one-sided and erroneous application of the directives of the Second Vatican Council, may have caused scandal and disturbance concerning the interpretation of the doctrine and the veneration due to this great sacrament. And I pray the Lord Jesus that in the future we may avoid in our manner of dealing with this sacred mystery anything which could weaken or disorient in any way the sense of reverence and love that exists in our faithful people.

"May Christ Himself help us to follow the path of true renewal toward that fullness of life and of Eucharistic worship whereby the Church is built up in that unity that she already possesses, and which she desires to bring to ever greater perfection for the glory of the living God and for the salvation of all humanity."

This pamphlet was compiled by Clementine Lenta

SECRETARIAT OF STATE

Vatican City
July 3, 1984

Dear Miss Lenta:

The Holy Father has directed me to acknowledge the letter and the Liturgical Directives pamphlet which you sent to him.

His Holiness appreciates the sentiments which prompted this devoted gesture and he wishes me to express his gratitude and to assure you of his prayers. He invokes upon you the peace and joy of Our Lord Jesus Christ and he cordially imparts his Apostolic Blessing.

Sincerely yours,

E. Martinez

Chapter Three

A Self Imposed Priest Shortage
From The Catholic World Report, November, 2000

**The alleged CRISIS in priestly vocations cannot be
separated from persistent complaints about
the plight of the orthodox seminarian**

By Michael S. Rose

One enduring subject in the landscape of Catholic America is popularly known as the "vocations crisis." Many will be familiar with this tale: Since the Second Vatican Council, the Church in the United States has seen fewer and fewer young men devoting themselves to the sacrificial life of the priesthood. Various reasons are given: materialism, practical and philosophical atheism, skepticism, subjectivism, individualism, hedonism, social injustice; parents who don't want their children to be priests; and the "unrealistic expectation" of lifelong celibacy.

While many of these factors have surely contributed to the dwindling number of Catholic priests in our now overwhelmingly secular society, these explanations may obscure the heart of the alleged vocations crisis. Parents, society, celibacy and materialism are inconclusive explanations for the declining number of priestly vocations.

In 1995 Archbishop Elden Curtiss, a former seminary rector and vocations director, penned an editorial for Omaha's diocesan newspaper, offering a refreshingly candid look at the vocations crisis:

> It seems to me that the vocation "crisis" is precipitated and continued by people who want to change the Church's agenda, by people who do not support orthodox candidates loyal to the magisterial teaching of the Pope and bishops, and by people who actually discourage viable candidates from seeking priesthood and vowed religious life as the Church defines these ministries.

Archbishop Curtiss made a second, equally interesting observation in his editorial:

> I am personally aware of certain vocations directors, vocations teams, and evaluation boards who turn away candidates who do not support the possibility of ordaining women or who defend the Church's teaching about artificial birth control, or who exhibit a strong piety toward certain devotions, such as the rosary.

If there is a determined effort to discourage these sorts of candidates from the priesthood, the shortage of priests that results is caused not by a lack of vocations but by deliberate attitudes and policies which effectively thwart true vocations.

Obstacles for the orthodox:

The words of Archbishop Curtiss have been confirmed by others time and again. In the course of researching a book that seeks to substantiate the archbishop's observations, this writer devoted a better part of the Jubilee year to interviewing dozens of seminarians, former seminarians, and recently ordained priests, representing 40 dioceses and 19 seminaries. In the four years before beginning that systematic research, I had spoken informally to numerous friends and acquaintances who had experience in seminaries. Each interviewee described himself as more or less representative of the "orthodox seminarian" to whom Archbishop Curtiss had alluded. These are men who are loyal to the teachings of the Church, look to the Pope as their spiritual father and leader, pray the rosary, and embrace the male, celibate priesthood.

It certainly must be acknowledged at the outset that not every candidate who enters a seminary has a genuine vocation to the priesthood. The seminary is a place designed to help a man to discern this vocation. Many eventually leave their studies because they have determined that a priestly vocation is not theirs. Others are rightly dismissed from the institutions due to irregularities that would indicate a particular man is not suited for the priesthood: sexual perversions, addictions, mental or emotional problems, incompetence, unwillingness to accept Church teaching, or lack of social or personal skills.

Insurmountable evidence, however, reveals that various other obstacles-man-made or "orchestrated," if you will—undermine authentic priestly vocations, leading to the orthodox seminarian's early dismissal or his voluntary departure (assuming he is admitted to a seminary program in the first place). Many of these circumstances owe their genesis to the seminary environment itself. So many orthodox seminarians, ex-seminarians and recently ordained priests have such remarkably similar stories to relate, the tales are difficult to dismiss as mere anecdotes.

Based on interviews I have conducted with 75 men and several seminary faculty members thus far, these stories, often accompanied by documented evidence, consistently reveal the same obstacles placed in the path of the orthodox candidate. These most commonly include the application screening process; psychological counseling; faculty members and spiritual directors who focus on detecting signs of orthodoxy among seminarians; a practical moral life of some students and faculty that is not compatible with the Christian standard; acceptance of homosexual practices and ideology; promotion of ideas and teachings which undermine Catholic belief in the most fundamental doctrines of the Church; disregard for proper liturgy and traditional devotions; and spiritual and psychological manipulation and abuse.

It appears that many of those in positions of authority at our seminaries are singularly motivated by a desire to redefine Catholic theology, the priesthood, and Church ministry according to their own "progressive" model. That model includes women priests, lay-run parishes, secularized worship, and a "soft" approach to Church doctrine; in other words, an emasculated, politically correct Church.

This "determined effort" (in the words of Archbishop Curtiss) to discourage priestly vocations among orthodox Catholics often involves a very similar pattern: the same characters, the same manipulative techniques, and the same injustices. Yet few bishops and priests have shown any willingness to heed the many complaints they have received about the process of priestly formation.

The disaffected orthodox seminarian is rarely supported in his grievances; he is often labeled as a troublemaker or a reactionary zealot, unfit for the priesthood. Once dismissed from one seminary he is blackballed from others, effectively lumped in with those who are potential sex offenders. Thus, once dismissed, it is difficult (though not always impossible) to be accepted into another seminary, diocese, or religious order.

The network of seminary rectors, psychologists, and priest-makers is a small and tight one. Communications are rapid and effective in purging the orthodox man from the seminary system. When the orthodox seminarian applies to transfer to another diocese, he is invariably asked whether he has ever been in seminary before. If the answer is affirmative, a call is immediately placed to the previous seminary, and a negative evaluation (from rector, psychologist, or spiritual director) is received. This applies not only to the seminarian who was formally expelled, but also to the one who left on his own initiative out of frustration or disgust.

The fact is that, for better or worse, a handful of people have extraordinary power to make or break many, many priestly vocations.

The Gatekeeper Phenomenon:

For some men, the road to ordination is cut short before it really begins. Even before a young man is ready to apply to a seminary, there are numerous forces that work against any possible priestly vocation he may be discerning. The feminization of the liturgy, poor catechesis, the example set by unmanly priests, and the many sexual scandals involving the clergy are four main deterrents for the discerning young man.

Once the young man has discerned that he would like to test his vocation in seminary, he applies to a diocese or religious order, naturally expecting that the institution will support his interest in the priesthood—especially in light of the ballyhooed "priest shortage." Many dioceses and religious orders, however, set up obstacles—although they may not acknowledge them as such—that deter the orthodox applicant from continuing to follow his call to the priesthood.

> If the screening process is not catching the deviates, is the process really designed to weed them out, or is it designed merely to prune the orthodox from the seminary vine?

For instance, applicants must often pass a litmus test on the subject of "what the Church should be." Often this means that the applicant must not let on that he accepts Church teaching on issues of authority and sexual morality, lest he be discarded as "rigid" or "dysfunctional." One of the most critical questions posed to potential seminarians, as Archbishop Curtiss indicated, is whether or not the applicant approves of priestly ordination for women. This question puts the orthodox seminarian in a difficult position. If he reveals that he agrees with the magisterium that the Church does not have the ability to ordain women, he is liable to be dismissed from further consideration. If he lies and says he is "open" to the idea, then he is no better than... well, a liar.

Although often it is the diocesan Vocations Director (usually a priest) who conducts the initial interview, it is also common that an assistant, usually a woman religious, serves as the inquisitor. One scenario—which would seem incredible, except that I heard similar stories from numerous seminarians—is that during an interview with the nun in the vocations office, the phone rings or there is a knock at the door. Sister answers and begins to engage in an animated conversation, in the course of which she states enthusiastically that she fully expects to be ordained to the priesthood in a matter of years, or otherwise makes it clear that she is a proponent of women's ordination. I personally have heard this sort of account (from various corners of the nation, and with a little variation in details) too many times to believe that the nuns were carrying on authentic conversations. This was a type of staged intimidation, which applicants to the more liberal dioceses were forced endure if they hoped to proceed to the priesthood. The nun was obviously trying to gauge the applicant's reaction. Many would-be seminarians elected to say, "No thanks," and end the process right there at the beginning, believing that the nun's actions were a reflection of the reigning attitudes in the diocese they were seeking "to serve."

Other inquisitors are not quite so dramatic in their questioning techniques, yet the results are essentially the same. It is a psychological game that often proves discouraging to vocations. And that is exactly the point.

In similar instances applicants are asked how they might respond to a hypothetical pastoral situation. For instance: If you were assigned to a parish in which the pastor was contravening Church law in the administration of his parish, what would you do? Or, if a man confessed to you that he and his wife have been using artificial contraception, but that they will continue to do so, would you give him absolution? Another popular hypothesis is framed this way:

What would you do if you were celebrating Mass at your new parish and a laywoman came up to concelebrate with you before the Eucharistic prayer?

Aside from the peculiarity of the questioning, such probing again puts the orthodox applicant at risk. How can he respond honestly without offending a vocations director who obviously wants to establish the applicant's "flexibility" or "open-mindedness" at the expense of Church teaching and discipline?

But this initial interview is only the beginning of a battery of evaluations and tests that are designed to weed out applicants who will not be suitable for a particular formation program. In many cases this process is an honest one. Proper screening of applicants for the priesthood is obviously of grave importance to the local Church. Unfortunately, this process is too often abused, and those who are sent away are those faithful to the teachings of the Church—especially those who properly accept the traditional role of the priest, including the commitment to lifelong celibacy. This is what I call the "gatekeeper phenomenon."

At the same time, despite the rigorous scrutiny applicants must pass through in order to enroll in a seminary program, all too many sexual deviates easily advance. There is no need to rehash the evidence on this issue in these pages. But one wonders: if the screening process is not catching the deviates, is the process really designed to weed them out, or is it designed merely to prune the orthodox from the seminary vine?

The psychological evaluation that is mandatory for each seminarian is also worthy of mention. A psychologist—who may not be Catholic or even Christian—probes the sexual and emotional history of a young man, often getting into a line of questioning that seems a tad perverted from the perspective of the average young man. It is not uncommon, for instance, for the psychologist to inquire about the applicant's beliefs on issues of homosexuality. Whereas one might understand this line of questioning if it were undertaken with an eye to root out those inclined to homosexuality or those who are involved in the gay lifestyle, the intent is more often a search to discover if the applicant is prepared to accept the practice of homosexuality. If the psychologist is not looking for an approbation of immoral acts, he at least would like to discover that the applicant is "open" in this regard.

And what happens if the young man is not ready to accept homosexuality? The orthodox applicant may well state Church teaching on homosexuality, saying that homosexual acts are intrinsically disordered and contrary to the natural law. But if he does, the psychologist is liable to report that the applicant has an "unhealthy sexuality," is "sexually immature," or has "sexual hangups." The applicant who is "open-minded," on the other hand, is deemed healthy and mature, with an "integrated sexuality."

The Gay Subculture:

If the applicant is accepted into a seminary program, he is liable to encounter homosexual issues many more times throughout his seminary career, sometimes in very direct ways. For years we have been hearing stories about sexual improprieties in our nation's seminaries, and these stories have effectively deterred many Catholic parents from encouraging a priestly vocation among their sons. The stories have, to be sure, dissuaded many young men from testing their vocations in certain dioceses. One book that is currently popular among priests and religious who have been advocating the elimination of mandatory clerical celibacy acknowledges the "gay subculture" in many of our seminaries. Written by Father Donald B. Cozzens, rector of St. Mary's Seminary in Cleveland, *The Changing Face of the Priesthood* warns of a growing public concern that the priesthood is becoming a "gay profession." The author spends considerable time addressing the issue from his perspective inside the seminary.

Father Cozzens states that "straight men in a predominantly or significantly gay environment commonly experience chronic destabilization, a common symptom of which is self-doubt." Compounding the challenge of studying, praying, and living alongside gay seminarians, he adds, "are seminary faculties which include a disproportionate number of homosexually oriented persons." In other words, this gay subculture, comprised of both students and faculty at certain seminaries, deters the healthy heterosexual man from continuing to study and prepare for the priesthood.

This is putting the issue mildly. How can any orthodox seminarian expect to be properly formed and prepared for the Catholic priesthood when he is constantly subjected to attitudes and behavior that are clearly contrary to Church teaching and discipline? How many heterosexual seminarians, whether orthodox or not, have decided to leave the seminary and abandon their vocations because of the gay subculture they were forced to confront—because they had been propositioned, harassed, or even molested? (One East Coast seminary is even nicknamed "The Pink Palace" because of its open acceptance of the gay subculture.)

And what becomes of those seminarians who stay? Seminary life can be made difficult for the "dissenting" seminarian: the one who does not condone sexual deviancy. I have heard many stories of seminarians being propositioned or harassed by fellow students and of faculty members who do not take their protests seriously. Last year, for instance, one seminarian was forced to procure a restraining order against a fellow student when his rector summarily dismissed his complaints that he was being sexually harassed by an "out-of-the-closet" gay classmate. The young man finally left that seminary, while gay seminarian who had been harassing him advanced in good standing.

Seminarians who accept the Church's teaching on sexual morality have also been threatened by classmates and faculty who have warned them that if they did not submit to homosexuality—at least to defend the normalcy of homosexual acts, if not actively to take part in them—their priestly careers would be in jeopardy. One seminary professor related to me how she was harassed by both students and fellow faculty members because of her overt acceptance of Church teaching on homosexuality. She became the focus of bitter condemnations even though her courses did not address the topic directly; one faculty colleague actually spat on her.

The orthodox seminarian is presented with another predicament in this regard: If there is something deviant or immoral going on at the seminary and he brings it to the attention of his superiors, he is likely risking expulsion. The members of seminary faculties usually do not appreciate students who go to their superiors with complaints especially about sexual foibles. One priest remarked of his seminary experience: "Many of my fellow students reminded me of the three monkeys: one with his hands over his eyes; one with his hands over his ears, and the other with his hands over his mouth." The maxim, "See no evil, hear no evil, speak no evil," seems to be a standard survival tactic in seminaries. That type of formation does not exactly prepare a seminarian to be a bold preacher of the Gospel. Nevertheless, that is the environment in which many priests are being formed today.

Doctrinal and Liturgical Abuses:

Beyond issues of personal immorality, the seminary environment presents a number of other problems for the orthodox seminarian. The most obvious and perhaps the most insidious is heterodoxy. Many faculty members have a terribly difficult time teaching what the Church teaches, and some even find it difficult to hide their disdain for Catholicism.

Some of the teachers who are entrusted with the formation of future priests do not support the Catholic priesthood as the Church defines it. In fact, they do not support the Church, her hierarchy, her Eucharist, or her liturgy.

All too often seminary faculty members assign textbooks written by noted dissenters from Catholic teaching—such as Richard McBrien, Edward Schillebeeckx, Hans Kung, or Charles Curran and parrot the dogmas of Catholic dissent. Those seminary students hear their instructors tell them that the Bible is "culture-bound," that one religion is as good as the next, that the Pope is not infallible, that the magisterium is abusive, that the Real Presence of Christ in the Eucharist is just a pre-Vatican II myth, that Christ was not really divine, that God is feminine, that the Mass is simply a communal meal, that women should be ordained priests in the name of equality, that homosexuality is normal, and that contraception is morally acceptable. This has been standard fare in many courses taught to our future priests over the past three decades or more. One former seminarian remarked on the content of the courses offered at his seminary: "The faculty followed everything from Pascendi Dominici Gregis down to the last detail." (He was referring to the encyclical in which Pope Pius X catalogued the errors of modernism.)

Yet many of the ideas being taught in seminaries today go well beyond the scope of even these familiar tenets of modernist ideology. Aggressive feminist theories are often put forth by religious sisters on the faculties. The widespread devotion to liberation theology and to various forms of Jungian psychology makes it clear that some of the teachers who are entrusted with the formation of future priests do not support the Catholic priesthood as the Church defines it. In fact, they do not support the Church, her hierarchy, her Eucharist, or her liturgy.

When the orthodox seminarian objects to false teachings, he is mocked and ridiculed for his "old-fashioned" views, called immature or infantile, and singled out for particularly harsh treatment. The desire for a "plurality of opinions"—a goal much espoused in seminaries today—stops short of a willingness to hear out the complaints of orthodox students.

Liturgical piety is used as another reason for discrimination against the orthodox seminarian. The powers-that-be in many seminaries have been perplexed over the past few years by the increasing demand by students for traditional devotions such as Eucharistic adoration, Benediction of the Blessed Sacrament, public rosary, and novenas. In response to this resurgence in traditional piety, the orthodox seminarians are often denied the opportunity for Eucharistic adoration, or forbidden to pray the rosary anywhere outside their own rooms. During Mass it is not uncommon for the celebrants, especially those who consider themselves "liturgists," to take great liberties with the liturgical rubrics. It is common, too, for seminarians to be forbidden to kneel at the proper parts of the Mass, such as during the Eucharistic prayer.

One priest said of his seminary days:

"It seems like they wanted to break us of any 'romantic notions' we may have had of how Mass ought to be celebrated." And he observed that this process continued even after his ordination, when, it seems, young orthodox priests were placed in parishes with liberal pastors who still fancied 1970s-style liturgical experimentation.

But liturgical abuses have effects far beyond offending the seminarian's sensibilities. They speak to the heart of the orthodox man studying for the priesthood. They speak of a crisis of authority and obedience, which all too often leads the seminarian to frustration and even contempt for his superiors. Unfortunately, this gets expressed in ways that are seen as "rigid" and "uncharitable."

Playing the Game:

The orthodox seminarian will naturally object to what he recognizes as false teachings or liturgical abuses, but once he does he has set himself up against the system, and it becomes increasingly difficult for him to advance toward ordination. Some young men are able to make it through the program—although they do not emerge unscathed—by writing on tests and answering in class what the professors want to hear. This tactic, to be sure, does not make for positive formation of courageous priests. First the students receive false teaching and observe illicit practices. Then they fall into the habit of saying what people want to hear, rather than what is true.

The seminarians who learn to "play the game" in this cynical way may actually emerge from the seminary worse equipped for their priestly ministry than their "open-minded" classmates. Although they may consider themselves orthodox, they have been programmed to accept a host of errors—if only by their silence. Nor can they be said to be well formed intellectually, no matter what they did outside the seminary to counteract the steady diet of dissident theology, secular ideology, and liturgical fads during their student career. Even if they do recognize some blatant errors in what they are taught, they may not ever learn the full truth.

Some seminarians are counseled to "play the game" just until they are ordained, so that then they can burst forth to defend the Church, the Pope, and the magisterium But rarely does this actually happen. Those who are ordained under such circumstances generally continue to "play the game" indefinitely—just as the politician who lies, cheats, and steals in order to gain office does not become an honest man once he takes the oath. After ordination, the young priest worries about getting a desirable parish assignment; years later the veteran priest worries about being given his own parish, being named a monsignor, or even being considered for episcopal appointment. "Playing the game" becomes a way of life, and invariably hinders the priest's ability to serve the faithful.

But what is the alternative to "playing the game?" When the honest seminarian challenges the professors, the rector, or any of his superiors (however charitably or tactfully he may do so), what can he expect? Often the seminarian is cast by his superiors as "mentally unbalanced." He may be administered a series of unfamiliar (and scientifically questionable) personality tests, on the basis of which he is diagnosed as "unstable" or even a "risk" candidate for the priesthood. He is then continuously reminded about this diagnosis whenever he does or says anything that is contrary to the positions of his dissident superiors. The orthodox seminarian may even be sent to psychological counseling to work out his problems of "rigidity" or his "authority problems."

Many young seminarians—if only because of their age—truly are idealistic and immature. So after being told over and over again that they are emotionally unstable, they might begin to believe the diagnosis themselves. In their immature reaction to their problems, they may actually begin to do and say odd things, which are then duly noted in their records as evidence to confirm the original diagnosis. Thus some seminaries not only teach dissident theology, but literally destroy the lives of those seminarians who have sought only to give themselves in service to the Church and to God. The result is that these men not only leave the seminaries, but sometimes they also lose their faith, or have serious residual emotional problems for a lifetime: problems that they did not have before entering the seminary.

A Self-imposed Crisis:

The net effect of discrimination against orthodox vocations to the priesthood is a shortage of priests. So this is essentially a self-imposed crisis.

More and more frequently, we hear reports by bishops warning of the coming crunch in priestly personnel within their dioceses. The problem they say, is that in the coming years there just will not be enough priests to serve the existing parishes. In November of last year, Bishop Thomas V. Daily of Brooklyn issued a pastoral letter addressing this issue. Proclaiming the priest shortage in his diocese "urgent and serious," he called for an increased emphasis on the parish "cluster" system through which neighboring churches could share resources and personnel—including a pastor.

Citing a problem with "burnout" and health problems among his overworked priests, Bishop James A. Griffin of Columbus, Ohio, issued guidelines last September to cope with the shortage of priests in his diocese. He reluctantly acknowledged that in the near future there may be no Mass on Sunday in a given parish. His guidelines address ways in which laity should respond to situations in which no priest is available, including celebrating Sunday and holy day liturgies without a priest.

In Green Bay, Wisconsin, Bishop Robert Banks projects that in five years only 20 to 25 of his 198 parishes will be "independent"—that is, having a pastor who is not shared with other parishes. These independent parishes are expected to have no fewer than 4,000 households each. Already 102 parishes share pastors and in some places a priest is responsible for as many as six parishes. Mark Mogilka, the chairman of Green Bay's diocesan planning committee, described the situation to the Green Bay Press-Gazette as a "paradigm shift in terms of what is leadership in the Catholic Church." Not surprisingly, the committee is focusing on forming "lay ministry teams" to replace priests.

The Diocese of Lexington, Kentucky, which recently completed a similar task-force evaluation, produced a plan in which deacons, nuns, and lay people will function as the heads of parishes. These "heads" will contract with priests for their sacramental services.

Thus priests will normally serve various parishes run by non-priests. In initial proposals published in the diocesan paper Crossroads the ordination of women and married men was considered.

While many American bishops have appointed task forces and planning commissions to study the projected shortage of priests, their proposed solutions invariably center around reducing the number of parishes served, rather than increasing the number of priests. So a great deal of time and energy is being expended on determining how we will get along without priests, rather than increasing the number of men entering into the priestly ministry. The results are closed parishes, parish mergers, and cluster arrangements in which the parishes are run by nuns and lay pastoral associates.

North of the border, Archbishop Marcel Gervais of Ottawa recently told the Ottawa Citizen that he has appointed lay men and women and nuns to officiate at marriages, baptisms, and funerals in his diocese, although these functions are specifically reserved to priests and deacons under the Church's canon law. His action comes after several years of appointing lay members and religious as "pastoral coordinators" of parishes. Archbishop Gervais touted his decision as "not just solving the problems" arising from a shortage of priests, but as "a new model of Church."

Indeed, there seems to be a discernible model, toward which many Catholic dissenters are deliberating striving: a lay-run Church with an emasculated priesthood.

In Saginaw, Michigan, under the leadership of Bishop Kenneth Untener (another former seminary rector), parishes are already commonly run by nuns and "lay pastors." One Michigan priest put it this way: "Bishop Untener done't think he needs priests. One guy comes to consecrate the hosts for a whole month and that's it for the duties of the priest." (It is instructive to note that Saginaw, with a Catholic population of 140,000, has averaged only one priestly ordination a year during the past decade.)

By contrast, those dioceses which have consistently promoted orthodoxy both in their parishes and in their seminaries have been affected little, if at all, by any "vocations crisis" or shortage of priests. Nor are the bishops of such dioceses issuing pastoral letters introducing parish "clusters" or giving instructions on how to celebrate the liturgy in the absence of a priest. Dioceses such as

Wichita, Lincoln, Arlington, Fargo, and Peoria have consistently been ordaining as many or more men each year than liberal dioceses five to ten times their size.

In the Rockford, Illinois diocese, for instance, Bishop Thomas Doran ordained eight priests last year: the highest number of ordinations there in 41 years. In Virginia, the Diocese of Arlington ordained 55 men to the priesthood in the years 1991–98. And the Diocese of Peoria, with a Catholic population of just 232,000 ordained 72 priests in the years 1991–98: an average of nine each year. In comparison, nearby Milwaukee, Wisconsin, with a Catholic population three times that of Peoria, ordained just two priests in 1998, while Detroit, with a Catholic population of 1.5 million (almost seven times that of Peoria) ordained an average of eight men each year from 1991–98.

Archbishop Curtiss' own Omaha archdiocese, considered one of the most conservative in the Midwest, ordained an average of seven men in the years from 1991–98 for a population of just 215,000 Catholics. Compare that to the Diocese of Madison, Wisconsin (with a slightly larger Catholic population), which ordained a total of four men during the entire period of 1991–98.

Other dioceses such as Denver and Atlanta, have turned their vocation programs around by actively supporting orthodox vocations and promoting fidelity to Church teaching, while emphasizing the traditional role of the priest as defined by the Church. Atlanta now has 61 seminarians, up from just nine in 1985. Denver boasted 68 seminarians in 1999, up from 26 in 1991. In addition to the Denver archdiocese's own current numbers, 20 more young men are studying for the Neocatechumenal Way and nine for other orders. All will serve the Archdiocese of Denver when ordained.

Fortunately, not all seminaries discriminate against orthodox vocations. Some, in fact, could be considered bastions of orthodoxy. Others it must be added, seem to want to move in that direction, although with entrenched ideologues on the faculty, It's a difficult task.

The Archdiocese of Denver has taken a unique approach to the issue of reforming a seminary. Several years ago then-Archbishop Francis Stafford bought St. Thomas Seminary after the Vincentian institution closed due to a dwindling student body. The problems, moral and pedagogical, were well known and documented. Last year Archbishop Charles Chaput, the present ordinary of Denver, re-opened the seminary under a new name and with a new faculty. St. John Vianney Theological Seminary is decidedly rooted in the theology of Pope John Paul II and Cardinal Joseph Ratzinger. Its faculty and students are overtly and joyfully supportive of the Catholic priesthood. Its mission is clearly to form holy and healthy priests for the "new evangelization." Rather than reading texts penned by dissidents who rose to notoriety the 1960s, the Vianney curriculum emphasizes the philosophy of St. Thomas Aquinas.

In August of 1998, Saint Gregory the Great College Seminary opened in the Diocese of Lincoln with an enrollment of 24, making it the first free-standing diocesan seminary to be opened in the United States for many decades. This year the 60-student seminary of the US branch of the Priestly Fraternity of St. Peter moved to the Diocese of Lincoln, which has always been considered one of the most conservative spots in the country. (In 1998, Lincoln boasted an amazing 44 seminarians for a diocese of just 85,000; the comparably sized Diocese of Covington, Kentucky, claimed only seven seminarians that year.)

Grasping the Solution?

His analysis may sound simplistic, but Archbishop Curtiss has outlined the solution to the problems that have beset our Catholic seminaries and vocations offices for the past four decades. He first recognizes that "orthodoxy breeds vocations." Then he candidly suggests that it is time to pay close attention to the dioceses which have been unaffected by the priest shortage or vocations crisis. If we are unwilling to recognize the reasons for their success, he says, "then we allow ourselves to become supporters of a self-fulfilling prophecy about the shortage of vocations."

The archbishop identifies the successful dioceses and religious orders as those that promote orthodoxy and loyalty to the Church, are unambiguous about the ordained priesthood as the Church defines that ministry, have bishops who are willing and able to confront dissent, and are willing to call forth candidates who share their loyalty to the Pope. "When this formula, based on total fidelity to Church teaching, is followed in dioceses and religious communities," he writes, "then vocations will increase."

The orthodox seminarian naturally wants to be supported in his vocation, not coerced into accepting theological opinions that the Church does not accept. He wants to be formed in an environment that does not hold him in contempt for his adherence to Church teaching and does not present obstacles to his growth in personal holiness. He wants to be surrounded by classmates and instructors who share his vision—which is not an idiosyncratic vision but the universal vision of the Church, working in unity for the salvation of souls.

Bishops would do well to take the advice of Archbishop Curtiss and look at successful dioceses and seminary programs to see what they are doing. They would do well to look to the dioceses which are not presently experiencing either a vocations crisis or a priest shortage. Reform of the nation's seminaries and vocations offices is a key. If that reform is not undertaken, the self-imposed priest shortage will occupy Catholic resources which would be better spent on evangelization, spiritual formation, and performing the spiritual and corporal works of mercy.

Michael S. Rose is editor of the St. Catherine Review and author of *The Renovation Manipulation*. He is currently writing a book on discrimination against orthodox vocations. He continues to seek research information pertinent to this topic. He can be reached at mrose@erinet.com

Chapter Four

Benefits of Eucharistic Adoration
John A. Hardon, S.J.
(Excerpt)

Experienced Benefits of Eucharistic Adoration.

The Council of Trent declared that Christ should be worshiped now in the Eucharist no less than He had been in first-century Palestine. Why? Because in the Blessed Sacrament "it is the same God Whom the apostles adored in Galilee" (*Decree on the Holy Eucharist*, chapter 5). The adorableness of the Eucharistic Christ, therefore, is an article of the Catholic faith.

What has become increasingly clear, however, is that Christ in the Eucharist is not only adorable but entreatable. He is not only to be adored, like Thomas did, by addressing Him as, "My Lord and my God." He is also to be asked for what we need, like the blind man who begged, "Lord, that I may see," or approached like the woman who said to herself, "If I can even touch His clothes, I shall be well again." By now countless believers have begged the Savior in the Eucharist for what they needed, and have come close to Him in the tabernacle or on the altar. Their resulting experience has profoundly deepened the Church's realization of how literally Christ spoke when He promised to be with us until the end of time.

The experience has been mainly spiritual: In giving light to the mind and strength to the will, in providing graces for oneself and others, in enabling weak human nature to suffer superhuman trials, in giving ordinary people supernatural power to accomplish extraordinary deeds.

Sts. John Fisher (1469–1535) and Thomas More (1478–1535) were strengthened in life and prepared themselves for martyrdom by fervent adoration of the Blessed Sacrament. In one of More's prayers, published after his death, we read, "0 sweet Saviour Christ, by the divers torments of Thy most bitter Passion, take from me, good Lord, this lukewarm fashion or rather key-cold meditation, and this dullness in praying to Thee. And give me Thy grace to long for Thy Holy Sacraments, and especially to rejoice in the Presence of Thy blessed Body, sweet Saviour Christ, in the Holy Sacrament of the Altar, and duly to thank Thee for Thy gracious visitation therewith."

St. Francis Xavier (1506–1552) after preaching and baptizing all day would often spend the night in prayer before the Blessed Sacrament.

St. Mary Magdalen de Pazzi (1566–1607) was a Carmelite nun from the age of seventeen. She recommended to busy people in the world to take time out each day for praying before the Holy Eucharist. "A friend," she wrote, "will visit a friend in the morning to wish him a good day, in the evening, a good night, taking also an opportunity to converse with him during the day. In like manner, make visits to Jesus Christ in the Blessed Sacrament, if your duties permit it. It is especially at the foot of the altar that one prays well. In all your visits to our Savior, frequently offer His precious Blood to the Eternal Father. You will find these visits very conducive to increase in you divine love.

St. Margaret Mary (1647–1680), a Visitation nun, found before the Blessed Sacrament the strength she needed to endure what witnesses at her beatification process declared were "contempt, contradictions, rebukes, insults, reproaches, without complaining, and praying for those by whom she was ill-treated."

It was Benedict XV who issued the first Code of Canon Law in 1917 which legislated the reservation of the Blessed Sacrament in "every parish or quasi-parish church, and in the church connected with the residence of exempt men and women religious" (Canon 1265, #1). It was this same Code which encouraged the private and public exposition of the Holy Eucharist.

Pope Pius XI associated the worship of Christ in the Blessed Sacrament with expiation for sin. St. Margaret Mary had been canonized in 1920, just two years before Achille Ratti was elected Pope. In 1928, he wrote a lengthy encyclical on Reparation to the Sacred Heart. Its whole theme is on the desperate need to plead for God's mercy, especially through the Holy Eucharist. During her prayers before the Blessed Sacrament, Christ revealed to Margaret Mary "the infinitude of His love, at the same time, in the manner of a mourner." The Savior said, "Behold this Heart which has loved men so much and has loaded them with all benefits, and for this boundless love has had no return but neglect and contumely, and this often from those who were bound by a debt and duty of a more special love." Among the ways to make reparation to the Heart of Christ, the Pope urged the faithful to "make expiatory supplications and prayers, prolonged for a whole hour—which is rightly called the 'Holy Hour' (*Miserentissimus Redemptor*, May 8, 1928). It was understood that the Holy Hour was to be made even as the original message was received by St. Margaret Mary, before the Holy Eucharist.

Pope Pius XII.

With Pius XI's successor, we begin a new stage in the Church's teaching on the efficacy of prayer addressed to Christ really present in the Sacrament of the altar.

A year before his election to the See of Peter, Cardinal Pacelli was sent as papal legate to the international Eucharistic Congress at Budapest in Hungary. It was 1938, a year before the outbreak of the Second World War. The theme of Pacelli's address at the Congress was that Christ had indeed left this earth in visible form at His Ascension. But He is emphatically still on earth, the Jesus of history, in the Sacrament of His love.

Pius XII published forty-one encyclicals during his almost twenty-year pontificate. One feature of these documents is their reflection of doctrinal development that has taken place in the Catholic Church in modern times. Thus, development in the Church's understanding of herself as the Mystical Body of Christ (*Mystici Corporis Christi*, 1943); in her understanding of the Bible (*Diving Afflante Spiritu*, 1943); in her understanding of the Blessed Virgin (*Deiparae Virginis Mariae*, 1946), proposing the definition of Mary's bodily Assumption into heaven.

The Encyclical *Mediator Dei* (1947) was on the Sacred Liturgy. As later events were to show, it became the doctrinal blueprint for the Constitution of the Liturgy of the Second Vatican Council.

Nine complete sections of *Mediator Dei* deal with "Adoration of the Eucharist." This provides the most authoritative explanation of what the Pope describes as "the worship of the Eucharist," which "gradually developed as something distinct from the Sacrifice of the Mass."

It seems best briefly to quote from these sections and offer some commentary.

1. *Adoration of the Eucharist.* The basis for all Eucharistic devotion is the fact that Christ in the Blessed Sacrament is the Son of God in human form.

The Eucharistic Food contains, as all are aware, "truly, really and substantially the Body and Blood together with the Soul and Divinity of Our Lord Jesus Christ." It is no wonder, then, that the Church, even from the beginning, adored the Body of Christ under the appearance of bread; this is evident from the very rites of the august Sacrifice, which prescribe that the sacred ministers should adore the Most Holy Sacrament by genuflecting or by profoundly bowing their heads.

The Sacred Councils teach that it is the Church's tradition right from the beginning, to worship "with the same adoration the Word Incarnate as well as His own flesh," and St. Augustine asserts that: "No one eats that flesh without first adoring it," while he adds that "not only do we not commit a sin by adoring it, but we do sin by not adoring it." (*Mediator Dei*, paragraph 129-130)

Everything else depends on this primary article of faith: that the Eucharist contains the living Christ, in the fullness of His human nature, and therefore really present under the sacred species; and in the fullness of His divine nature, and therefore to be adored as God.

2. *Dogmatic Progress.* There has been a deeper grasp by the Church of every aspect of the mystery of the Eucharist. But one that merits special attention is the growing realization, not only of Christ's sacrificial oblation in the Mass, but of His grace-filled presence outside of Mass.

It is on this doctrinal basis that the worship of adoring the Eucharist was founded and gradually developed as something distinct from the Sacrifice of the Mass. The reservation of the Sacred Species for the sick and those in danger introduced the praiseworthy custom of adoring the Blessed Sacrament which is reserved in our Churches. This practice of adoration, in fact, is based on strong and solid reasons. For the Eucharist is at once a Sacrifice and a Sacrament: but it differs from the other Sacraments in this—that it not only produces grace, but contains, in a permanent manner, the Author of grace Himself. When, therefore, the Church bids us adore Christ hidden behind the Eucharistic veils and pray to Him for the spiritual and temporal favors of which we ever stand in need, she manifests living faith in her divine Spouse who is present beneath these veils, she professes her gratitude to Him and she enjoys the intimacy of His friendship. (131)

The key to seeing why there should be a Eucharistic worship distinct from the Mass is that the Eucharist is Jesus Christ. No less than His contemporaries in Palestine adored and implored Him for the favors they needed, so we should praise *and* thank Him, and implore Him for what we need.

3. Devotional Development. As a consequence of this valid progress in doctrine, the Church has developed a variety of Eucharistic devotions.

Now, the Church in the course of centuries has introduced various forms of this worship which are ever increasing in beauty and helpfulness; as, for example, visits of devotion to the tabernacle, even every day, Benediction of the Blessed Sacrament; solemn processions, especially at the time of Eucharistic Congresses, which pass through cities and villages; and adoration of the Blessed Sacrament publicly exposed. Sometimes these public acts of adoration are of short duration. Sometimes they last for one, several and even for forty hours. In certain places they continue in turn in different churches throughout the year, while elsewhere adoration is perpetual, day and night (132).

To be stressed is that these are not merely passing devotional practices. They are founded on divinely revealed truth. And, as the Pope is at pains to point out, "these exercises of piety have brought a wonderful increase in faith and supernatural life to the Church militant upon earth."

Are these practices liturgical? "They spring from the inspiration of the Liturgy," answers Pius XII. "And if they are performed with due decorum and with faith and piety, as the liturgical rules of the Church require, they are undoubtedly of the very greatest assistance in living the life of the Liturgy.

Does this not confuse the "Historic Christ" with the Eucharistic Christ? Not at all, says the Pope.

On the contrary, it can be claimed that by this devotion the faithful bear witness to and solemnly avow the faith of the Church that the Word of God is identical with the Son of the Virgin Mary, Who suffered on the Cross, Who is present in a hidden manner in the Eucharist and Who reigns upon His heavenly throne. Thus St. John Chrysostom states: "When you see It (the Body of Christ) exposed, say to yourself: thanks to this Body, I am no longer dust and ashes, I am no more a captive but a freeman: hence I hope to obtain Heaven and the good things that are there in store for me, eternal life, the heritage of the Angels, companionship with Christ" (134).

Among other forms of Eucharistic devotion recommended by Pope Pius XII, he gave special attention to Benediction of the Blessed Sacrament. He spoke of the "great benefit in that custom which makes the priest raise aloft the Bread of Angels before congregations with heads bowed down in adoration and forming with It the sign of the cross." This "implores the Heavenly Father to deign to look upon His Son who for love of us was nailed to the Cross and for His sake and through Him willed . . . to shower down heavenly favors upon those whom the Immaculate Blood of the Lamb has redeemed" (135).

Pope John XXIII.

Unlike his predecessor, John XXIII did not publish any extensive documentation on the Eucharistic Liturgy. But he took every occasion to urge the faithful, especially priests, to pray before the Blessed Sacrament.

In the life of a priest nothing could replace the silent and prolonged prayer before the altar. The adoration of Jesus, our God; thanksgiving, reparation for our sins and for those of all men, the prayer for so many intentions entrusted to Him, combine to raise that priest to a greater love for the Divine Master to whom he has promised faithfulness and for men who depend on his priestly ministry.

With the practice of this enlightened and fervent worship of the Eucharist, the spiritual life of the priest increases and there are prepared the missionary energies of the most valuable apostles.

All the while that he was urging priests to pray before the altar, the Pope reminded them that "the Eucharistic Prayer in the full sense is the Holy Sacrifice of the Mass" (Encyclical *Sacerdotii Nostri Primordia*, August 11, 1959). After all, without the Mass there would be no Real Presence. We might say that Christ's abiding presence in the Holy Eucharist is an extension of the Eucharistic sacrifice.

On the eve of the Second Vatican Council, Pope John participated in the Corpus Christi procession of the Blessed Sacrament in Rome. On that occasion, he composed an earnest prayer for Christ's blessings on the forthcoming Council.

O Jesus, look upon us from your Sacrament like a good Shepherd, by which name the Angelic Doctor invokes you, and with him Holy Church. O Jesus, good Shepherd, this is your flock, the flock that you have gathered from the ends of the earth, the flock that listens to your word of life, and intends to guard it, practice it and preach it. This is the flock that follows you meekly, O Jesus, and wishes so ardently to see, in the Ecumenical Council, the reflection of your loving face in the features of your Church, the mother of all, the mother who opens her arms and heart to all, and here awaits, trembling and trustful, the arrival of all her Bishops (June 21, 1962).

Words could not be plainer. They could also not be more authoritative. The Vicar of Christ was teaching, by example, how effective prayer to our Lord in the Eucharist can be not only for ourselves personally, but for the whole Church of God.

Pope Paul VI.

Although Pope John XXIII opened the Second Vatican Council and lived through its first session in 1962, he did not promulgate any of its sixteen documents. That was done by his successor, Pope Paul VI.

The first conciliar document issued by Paul VI was the *Constitution on the Sacred Liturgy* (December 4, 1963). Less than two years later, just before the last session of the Council, he published the encyclical *Mysterium Fidei* (September 3, 1965). It is a remarkable document in several ways.

- It was issued during the Second Vatican Council.

- It opens with a glowing tribute to the Council's Constitution on the Liturgy.

- It praises those who "seek to investigate more profoundly and to understand more fruitfully the doctrine on the Holy Eucharist."

But then it goes on to give "reasons for serious pastoral concern and anxiety." Specifically, Paul VI says that opinions are being spread which reinterpret "doctrine already defined by the Church," and in particular "the dogma of transubstantiation." (I)

Most of the encyclical, therefore, is a doctrinal analysis of the Real Presence. By all accounts, it is the most extensive and penetrating declaration in papal history on two articles of the Catholic faith: the corporeal presence of Jesus Christ in the Blessed Sacrament and His communication of grace through this Eucharistic presence now on earth.

1. The Real Presence. If we are to understand the sacramental presence of Christ in the Eucharist, "which constitutes the greatest miracle of its kind, we must listen with docility to the voice of the teaching and praying Church." What does the doctrine and devotion of the Church tell us? This voice, which constantly echoes the voice of Christ, assures us that the way Christ is made present in this Sacrament is none other than by the change of the whole substance of the bread into His Body, and of the whole substance of the wine into His Blood, and that this unique and truly wonderful change the Catholic Church rightly calls transubstantiation. As a result of transubstantiation, the species of bread and wine undoubtedly take on a new meaning and a new finality, for they no longer

remain ordinary bread and ordinary wine, but become the sign of something sacred, the sign of a spiritual food. However, the reason they take on this new significance and this new finality is simply because they contain a new reality which we may justly term onto-logical. There is no longer under the species what had been there before. It is something entirely different. Why? Not only because of the faith of the church, but in objective reality. After the change of the substance or nature of the bread and wine into the Body and Blood of Christ, nothing remains of the bread and wine but the appearances, under which Christ, whole and entire, in His physical reality is bodily present (V).

Of course this presence is beyond our comprehension. Of course it is different from the way bodies are naturally present and there-fore can be sensibly perceived. Subjectively, we cannot see or touch the Body of Christ in the Eucharist. But objectively (in reality) and ontologically (in His being) He is there.

2. Communication of Grace. Once the Real Presence is properly recognized, it is only logical to conclude that we should worship the Savior in the Blessed Sacrament. It is equally logical to expect Him to confer blessings on a sinful world by His presence among us. Three passages in *Mysterium Fidei* make this conclusion per-fectly clear.

In the first statement, Pope Paul recalls the teaching of St. Cyril of Alexandria (died 444) who had been so active in defending the physical union of Christ's humanity in the Incarnation as well as in the Eucharist. The reason is that the Eucharist is the Incarnate Son of God who became, and remains, the Son of Mary.

St. Cyril of Alexandria rejects as folly the opinion of those who maintained that if a part of the Eucharist was left over for the following day, it did not confer sanctification. "For" he says, "nei-ther Christ is altered nor His Holy Body changed, but the force and power and revivifying grace remain with it" (VI).

Once the elements of bread and wine have been consecrated and transubstantiation has taken place, the living Christ remains as long as the Eucharistic species remain. Then, because Christ is present, His humanity remains a source of life-giving grace.

In his second statement on the Eucharist as a channel of grace,

Pope Paul carefully distinguishes between the Eucharist as Sacrifice and Communion, and the Eucharist as Presence.

Not only while the Sacrifice is offered and the Sacrament is received, but as long as the Eucharist is kept in our churches and oratories, Christ is truly the Emmanuel, that is "God with us." Day and night He is in our midst, He dwells with us, full of grace and truth. He restores morality, nourishes virtues, consoles the afflicted and strengthens the weak (VI).

These verbs—restores, nourishes, consoles and strengthens—are all forms of divine grace which Christ confers by His presence in the Eucharist. In his third statement on the efficacy of the Real Presence, Paul VI adds the final touch to his teaching. No doubt the living Savior in the Blessed Sacrament is there "full of grace and truth." But there must be a responsive faith on our part.

Anyone who approaches this august Sacrament with special devotion, and endeavors to return generous love for Christ's own infinite love, will experience and fully understand—not without spiritual joy and fruit—how precious is the life hidden with Christ in God, and how great is the value of converse with Christ. For there is nothing more consoling on earth, nothing more efficacious for advancing along the road of holiness (VI).

The important word in that last sentence is "efficacious." Provided we approach the Real Presence with believing love, Christ will perform wonders of His grace in our lives.

Pope John Paul II.

Building on the teaching of his predecessors, John Paul II has come to be known as the Pope of the Real Presence. In one document and address after another, he has repeated what needs repetition for the sake of emphasis: "The Eucharist, in the Mass and outside of the Mass, is the Body and Blood of Jesus Christ, and is therefore deserving of the worship that is given to the living God, and to Him alone." (Opening address in Ireland, Phoenix Park, September 29, 1979)

But the Pope has done more than merely repeat what had been said before. He placed the capstone on the Eucharistic teaching of the magisterium that we have been examining. He did so by explaining in the most unambiguous language that there is only one Sacrament of the Eucharist. Yet this one Sacrament confers grace in three different ways. Each manner of giving grace corresponds to the three forms in which the Eucharist has been instituted by Christ.

It is at one and the same time a Sacrifice-Sacrament, a Communion-Sacrament, and a Presence-Sacrament: (Encyclical *Receptor Hominis*, March 4, 1979, IV, 20)

The revealed foundation for this conclusion is the fact of Christ's abiding presence in the Eucharist. It is the "Redeemer of Man" who by His Passion and death on the Cross merited the grace of our salvation. But it is mainly through the Eucharist that the same Jesus Christ now channels this grace to a sinful human race.

It is in this comprehensive sense that we can say, "the Church lives by the Eucharist, by the fullness of this Sacrament." This fullness, however, spans all three levels of its sacramental existence, where by "sacrament" the Church means a sensible sign, instituted by Christ, through which invisible grace and inward sanctification are communicated to the soul.

The Mass is the Sacrifice-Sacrament of the Eucharist. As the Council of Trent declared, the Sacrifice of the Mass is not only an offering of praise and thanksgiving. It is also a source of grace: "By this oblation, the Lord is appeased, He grants grace and the gift of repentance, and He pardons wrongdoings and sins," the blessings of Redemption which Christ won for us by His bloody death on Calvary are now "received in abundance through this unbloody oblation." (September 17, 1562)

Liturgical Abuse, *A Cancer in the Church*

Chapter Five

Modernism and Liberalism

The heresy called Modernism is now rampant within the Church. St. Pius X had challenged this heresy in his Pontificate and stopped it dead in its tracks. But with the unchallenged power of the liberal element of bishops and theologians during and after Vatican Council II, this heresy seems now to be stronger than ever. Vatican II is not, however, the cause of the current problems in the Church. The Modernists and the liberal bishops rather, choose to misinterpret it and claim that the changes they inaugurate in all aspects of the Faith are the intent of the Council. They could not be more in error but they are and have been very successful in accomplishing their agenda.

Those in the Church who keep a close eye on developments recognize that the Modernists are still operating in the exact manner they operated in St. Pius X's time, but little or no success from the Vatican on down through the hierarchy has taken place because nothing like the warfare Pius X waged is going on now or since the Council ended in 1965.

On May 10, 2000 the National Council of Catholic Bishops authoritatively announced that "Catholics For A Free Choice" merits no recognition or support as a Catholic organization. Let us hope that "Call To Action" will soon receive the same attention from the Council.

The frustration of Catholics who are loyal to the Magisterium has become a real cross to bear and a challenge to their faith. There are two generations of Catholics out there who know little about the Faith and are therefore impotent in recognizing the various changes and movements that are weakening and threatening the whole Church, and subsequently they do nothing to counter the progress of the "bad-guys." I can hear someone crying out this moment in complaint because this author has resorted to the use of terms like liberal, conservative, and modernist. When you read the following words of St. Pius X in his description of the modernists and their mode of operation, you might agree that we really need some name to hang on the rascals in order to identify even broadly their shenanigans and intentions. It's hard to fight against a target unless you can recognize it. Here are pertinent excerpts for those of you who want to understand more about the biggest threat to the Church today and how it makes in-roads into every facet of the Church we love. . .

Every Catholic should be familiar with the following description of the Modernist by Pope Pius X, so that he/she can identify these heretics as wolves in sheep clothing, destroying the Church from within.

From the Encyclical Pascendi Dominici Gregis
By St. Pius X

The Identification and Condemnation of Modernism
(Excerpts:)

". . . It may perhaps be asked how is it that this need of the divine which man experiences within himself resolves itself into religion? To this question the Modernist reply would be as follows: Science and history are confined within two boundaries, the one external, namely, the visible world, the other internal, which is the consciousness. When one or the other of these limits has been reached, there can be no further progress, for beyond is the unknowable. In the presence of this unknowable, whether it is outside man and beyond the visible world of nature, or lies hidden within the subconsciousness, the need of the divine in a soul which is prone to religion excites. . . a certain sense, and this sense possesses, implied within itself both as its own object and as its intrinsic cause, the divine realty itself, and in a way unites man with god. It is this sense to which the Modernists give the name of faith, and this is what they hold to be the beginning of religion.

"But we have not yet reached the end of their philosophizing, or, to speak more accurately, of their folly. Modernists find in this sense not only faith, but in and with faith, as they understand it, they affirm that there is also to be found revelation. For, indeed, what more is needed to constitute a revelation? Is not that religious sense which is perceptible in the conscience, revelation, or at least the beginning of revelation? Nay, is it not God Himself manifesting Himself, indistinctly, it is true, in this same religious sense to the soul? And they add: Since God is both the object and the cause of faith, this revelation is at the same time of God and from God, that is to say, God is both the Revealer and the Revealed.

"From this, Venerable Brethren, springs that most absurd tenet of the Modernists, that every religion, according to the different aspect under which it is viewed, must be considered as both natural and supernatural. It is thus that they make consciousness and revelation synonymous. From this they derive the law laid down as the universal standard, according to which religious consciousness is to be put on an equal footing with revelation, and that to it all must submit, even the supreme authority of the church, whether in the capacity of teacher, or in that of the legislator in the province of sacred liturgy or discipline.

". . . Thus it is evident that science is to be entirely independent of faith, while on the other hand, and not withstanding that they are supposed to be strangers to each other, faith is made subject to science. All this, Venerable Brothers, is in formal opposition to the teachings of our predecessor, Pius IX, where he lays it down that "In matters of religion it is the duty of philosophy not to command but to serve, not to prescribe what is to be believed, but to embrace what is to be believed with reasonable obedience, not to scrutinize the depths of the mysteries of God, but to venerate them devoutly and humbly.'

"[The Modernists] lay down the general principle that in a living religion everything is subject to change, and must in fact be changed. In this way they pass to what is practically their principal doctrine, namely, evolution. To the laws of evolution everything is subject to change under penalty of death—dogma, Church, worship, the Books we revere as sacred, even faith itself.

". . .With all this in mind, one understands how it is that the Modernists express astonishment when they are reprimanded or punished. What is imputed to them as a fault they regard as a sacred duty. They understand the needs of consciences better than anyone else, since they come into closer touch with them than does the ecclesiastical authority. . . Let authority rebuke them if it pleases—they have their own consciences on their side and an intimate experience which tells them with certainty that what they deserve is not blame but praise. . . . And thus they go their way, reprimands and rebukes not withstanding, masking an incredible audacity under a mock semblance of humility. While they make a pretense of bowing their heads, their minds and hands are more boldly intent than ever on carrying out their purposes. And this policy they follow willingly and wittingly both because it is part of their system that authority is to be stimulated but not dethroned, and because it is necessary for them to remain within the ranks of the Church in order that they may gradually transform the collective conscience. And in saying this, they fail to perceive that they are avowing that the collective conscience is not with them, and that they have no right to claim to be its interpreters.

". . . It remains for us now to say a few words about the Modernist as reformer. From all that has preceded, it is abundantly clear how great and how eager is the passion of such men for innovation. In all Catholicism there is absolutely nothing on which it does not fasten. They wish philosophy to be reformed, especially in the ecclesiastical seminaries. . . Dogmas and their evolution are to be harmonized with science and history. In the Catechism no dogmas are to be inserted except those that have been reformed and are within the capacity of the people. Regarding worship they say, the number of external devotions is to be reduced, and steps taken to prevent their further increase, though, indeed, some of the admirers of symbolism are disposed to be indulgent on this head. . . They cry out that ecclesiastical government requires to be reformed in all its branches, but especially in its disciplinary and dogmatic departments. They insist both outwardly and inwardly it must be brought into harmony with the modern conscience which now wholly tends towards democracy; a share in ecclesiastical government should therefore be given to the lower ranks of the clergy and even to the laity and authority which is too much concentrated should be decentralized.

". . .They ask that the clergy should. . . in their ideas and actions, admit the principles of Modernism and there are some, who gladly listening to the teaching of their Protestant masters, would desire the suppression of the celibacy of the clergy. What is left in the Church which is not to be reformed by them according to their principles?...We have already intimated their system means the destruction not of the catholic church alone, but of all religion. Hence the rationalists are not wanting in their applause, and the most frank among them congratulate themselves on having found in the Modernists the most valuable of allies.

". . . But it is pride which exercises an incomparably greater sway over the soul to blind it and lead it into error, and pride sits in Modernism as in its own house, finding sustenance everywhere in its doctrine and lurking in its every aspect. It is pride which fills Modernists with that self-assurance by which they consider themselves and pose as the rule for all. It is pride that puffs them up with that vainglory which allows themselves as the sole possessors of knowledge, and makes them say, elated and inflated with presumption, "We are not as the rest of men," and which, lest they should seem as other men, leads them to embrace and to devise novelties even of the most absurd kind. IT IS PRIDE WHICH AROUSES IN THEM THE SPIRIT OF DISOBEDIENCE and causes them to demand a compromise between authority and liberty. It is owing to their pride that they seek to be reformers of others while they forget to reform themselves, and that they are found to be utterly wanting in respect for authority, even for the supreme authority. Truly, there is no road which leads more directly and so quickly to Modernism as pride.

"When a Catholic layman or a priest forgets the precept of the Christian life which obliges us to renounce ourselves if we would follow Christ and neglects to tear pride from his heart, then it is he who most of all is a fully ripe subject for the errors of Modernism. For this reason, Venerable Brethren, it will be your first duty to resist such victims of pride, to employ them only in the lowest and most obscurest offices. The higher they try to rise, the lower let them be placed, so that the lowliness of their position may limit their power of causing damage. Examine most carefully your young clerics by yourselves and by the directors of your SEMINARIES, and when you find the spirit of pride among them reject them without compunction from the priesthood. Would to God that this had always been done with vigilance and constancy which were required.

They [the Modernists] exercise all their ingenuity in an effort to weaken the force and falsify the character of tradition, so as to rob it of all its weight and authority. . . Finally the Modernists try in every way to diminish and weaken the authority of the ecclesiastical magisterium itself by sacrilegiously falsifying its origin, character, and rights, and by freely repeating the calumnies of its adversaries. . . This being so, there is little reason to wonder that the Modernists vent all their bitterness and hatred on Catholics who zealously fight the battles of the Church.

". . . What efforts do they not make to win new recruits! They seize upon professorships in the seminaries and universities, and gradually make of them chairs of pestilence. In sermons from the pulpit they disseminate their doctrines, although possibly in utterances which are veiled. . . We have to deplore the spectacle of many young men, once full of promise and capable of rendering great services to the Church, now gone astray.

". . . All these prescriptions, both our own and those of our predecessor, are to be kept in view whenever there is question of choosing directors and professors for seminaries and catholic Universities. Anyone who in any way is found to be tainted with Modernism is to be exclude without compunction from these offices, whether of government or of teaching, and those who already occupy them are to be removed.

". . . The same policy is to be adopted towards those who openly or secretly lend countenance to Modernism either by extolling the Modernists and excusing their culpable conduct, or by carping at scholasticism, and the Fathers, and the magisterium of the Church, or by refusing obedience to ecclesiastical authority in any of its depositories, and towards those who show a love of novelty in history, archaeology, biblical exegesis; and finally towards those who neglect the sacred sciences or appear to prefer them to the secular. . . Strong in the consciousness of your duty, act always in this matter with prudence and vigor."

(End of excerpts from the encyclical)

Commentary

The reader must certainly have recognized from the above that St. Pius X had identified every one of the problems that also exist in the Church today. His emphasis on disobedience of some of the clergy, his discussion on the connection between pride and Modernism, and the persecution of those remaining loyal to the traditions of the Church and the Magisterium can all be recognized as described by Mr. Michael Rose in his essay "A Self Imposed Shortage," in Chapter Two, in which he describes what is taking place in some of our seminaries and dioceses.

It is obvious that the warnings and guidance imposed upon the bishops in 1905 has fallen by the wayside today and Modernism has again become deeply entrenched within the Church. This major heresy is tearing the Church apart and, as had been predicted by the Virgin Mary at Akita, Japan, bishop has turned against bishop, and priest against priest. The laity is in a turmoil of confusion because of groups like Call To Action; Catholics For a Free Choice, rebellious nuns, and seminaries that lack proper leadership. The sad observation today is the appearance that very little organized action is being taken to counteract the Modernists. They manage to have it both ways—that is, they remain in the Church professing to be loyal members, while at the same time they undermine its teachings at every opportunity while remaining undetected as to who they really are and what they truly profess.

The Catholic laity can be of great service to the Church if the orthodox believers take action to challenge liturgical abuses and follow the guidelines in Chapters Two and Three in reporting them through the proper ecclesiastical channels with courtesy and respect, but also with the conviction that their rights are being exercised under the law of the Church.

The gates of Hell will not prevail against this Church but every Catholic loyal to the Magisterium must support those bishops who are loyal to the Church. The laity now needs to take the proper steps to influence a change in current conditions. The New Springtime for the Church will come but it appears that it is still a long, long way off. But God is in His heaven and the purification of the Church will definitely take place one day.

Prayer, sacrifice, fasting, prudent action, a reformation of the seminaries, and support of the orthodox bishops and priests by traditional Catholics is the answer.

Chapter Six

Mysterium Fidei
Encyclical on the Holy Eucharist
Promulgated on September 3, 1965
His Holiness Pope Paul VI

To our venerable brothers, the Patriarchs, Primates, Archbishops, Bishops and other local Ordinaries in peace and communion with the Holy See, and to all the clergy and faithful of the world.

Venerable brothers and dear Sons:
Health and apostolic benediction.

THE CATHOLIC CHURCH has always devoutly guarded as a most precious treasure the mystery of faith, that is, the ineffable gift of the Eucharist which she received from Christ her Spouse as a pledge of His immense love, and during the Second Vatican Council in a new and solemn demonstration she professed her faith and veneration for this mystery. When dealing with the restoration of the sacred liturgy, the Fathers of the council, by reason of their pastoral concern for the whole Church, considered it of the highest importance to exhort the faithful to participate actively with sound faith and with the utmost devotion in the celebration of this Most Holy Mystery, to offer it with the priest to God as a sacrifice for their own salvation and for that of the whole world, and to find in it spiritual nourishment.

For if the sacred liturgy holds the first place in the life of the Church, the Eucharistic Mystery stands at the heart and center of the liturgy, since it is the font of life by which we are cleansed and strengthened to live not for ourselves but for God, and to be united in love among ourselves.

To make evident the indissoluble bond which exists between faith and devotion, the Fathers of the council, confirming the doctrine which the Church has always held and taught and which was solemnly defined by the Council of Trent, determine to introduce their treatise on the Most Holy Mystery of the Eucharist with the following summary of truths:

> "At the Last Supper, on the night He was handed over,
> Our Lord instituted the Eucharistic Sacrifice of His Body
> and Blood, to perpetuate the sacrifice of the cross through-
> out the ages until He should come, and thus entrust to the
> Church, His beloved spouse, the memorial of His death
> and resurrection: a sacrament of devotion, a sign of unity,
> a bond of charity, a paschal banquet in which Christ is
> received, the soul is filled with grace and there is given to
> us the pledge of future glory." [1]

In these words are highlighted both the sacrifice, which pertains to the essence of the Mass which is celebrated daily, and the
sacrament in which the faithful participate in Holy Communion by
eating the Flesh of Christ and drinking His Blood, receiving both
grace, the beginning of eternal life, and the medicine of immortal-
ity. According to the words of Our Lord: "The man who eats my
flesh and drinks my blood enjoys eternal life, and I will raise him
up at the last day."[2]

Therefore we earnestly hope that the restored sacred liturgy
will bring forth abundant fruits of eucharistic devotion, so that the
Holy Church, under this saving sign of piety, may make daily
progress toward perfect unity [3] and may invite all Christians to a
unity of faith and of love, drawing them gently, thanks to the action
of divine grace.

We seem to have a preview of these fruits and, as it were, to
gather in the early results not only in the genuine joy and eagerness
with which the members of the Catholic Church have received both
the Constitution on the Sacred Liturgy and the restoration of the
liturgy, but also in the great number of well-prepared publications
which seek to investigate more profoundly and to understand more
fruitfully the doctrine on the Holy Eucharist, with special reference to its relation with the mystery of the Church.

All of this is for us a cause of profound consolation and joy. It
is a great pleasure for us to communicate this to you, venerable
brothers, so that along with us you may give thanks to God, the
giver of all gifts, who with His Spirit rules the Church and enriches

her with increasing virtues.

REASONS FOR PASTORAL CONCERN AND ANXIETY

However, venerable brothers, in this very matter which we are discussing, there are not lacking reasons for serious pastoral concern and anxiety. The awareness of our apostolic duty does not allow us to be silent in the face of these problems. Indeed, we are aware of the fact that, among those who deal with this Most Holy Mystery in written or spoken word, there are some who, with reference either to Masses which are celebrated in private, or to the dogma of transubstantiation, or to devotion to the Eucharist, spread abroad opinions which disturb the faithful and fill their minds with no little confusion about matters of faith. It is as if everyone were permitted to consign to oblivion doctrine already defined by the Church, or else to interpret it in such a way as to weaken the genuine meaning of the words or the recognized force of the concepts involved.

To confirm what we have said by examples, it is not allowable to emphasize what is called the "communal" Mass to the disparagement of Masses celebrated in private, or to exaggerate the element of sacramental sign as if the symbolism, which all certainly admit in the Eucharist, expresses fully and exhausts completely the mode of Christ's presence in this sacrament. Nor is it allowable to discuss the mystery of transubstantiation without mentioning what the Council of Trent stated about the marvelous conversion of the whole substance of the bread into the Body and of the whole substance of the wine into the Blood of Christ, speaking rather only of what is called "transignification" and "transfiguration," or finally to propose and act upon the opinion according to which, in the Consecrated Hosts which remain after the celebration of the sacrifice of the Mass, Christ Our Lord is no longer present.

Everyone can see that the spread of these and similar opinions does great harm to the faith and devotion to the Divine Eucharist.

And therefore, so that the hope aroused by the council, that a flourishing of eucharistic piety which is now pervading the whole Church, be not frustrated by this spread of false opinions, we have with apostolic authority decided to address you, venerable brothers, and to express our mind on this subject.

We certainly do not wish to deny in those who are spreading these singular opinions the praiseworthy effort to investigate this lofty mystery and to set forth its inexhaustible riches, revealing its meaning to the men of today; rather we acknowledge and approve their effort. However, we cannot approve the opinions which they express, and we have the duty to warn you about the grave danger which these opinions involve for correct faith.

THE HOLY EUCHARIST IS A MYSTERY OF FAITH

First of all we wish to recall something which is well known to you but which is altogether necessary for repelling every virus of rationalism, something to which many illustrious martyrs have witnessed with their blood, while celebrating Fathers and Doctors of the Church constantly professed and taught it; that is, that the Eucharist is a very great mystery. In fact, properly speaking, and to use the words of the sacred liturgy, it is the Mystery of Faith. "Indeed, in it alone," as Leo XIII our predecessor of happy memory very wisely remarked, "are contained, in a remarkable richness and variety of miracles, all supernatural realities." [4]

We must therefore approach especially this mystery with humble respect, not following human arguments, which ought to be silent, but adhering firmly to divine revelation.

St. John Chrysostom, who, as you know, treated of the eucharistic mystery with such nobility of language and insight born of devotion, instructing his faithful on one occasion about this mystery, expressed these most fitting words:

> "Let us submit to God in all things and not contradict Him, even if what He says seems contrary to our reason and intellect; rather let His words prevail over our reason and intellect. Let us act in this way with regard to the (eucharistic) mysteries, looking not only at what falls under our senses but holding on to His words. For His word cannot lead us astray."[5]

The scholastic Doctors often made similar affirmations: That in this sacrament are the true Body of Christ and His true Blood is something that "cannot be apprehended by the senses," says St. Thomas, "but only by faith which relies on divine authority. This is why, in a comment on Luke 22:19 ('This is My Body which is given for you'), St. Cyril says: 'Do not doubt whether this is true, but rather receive the words of the Savior in faith, for since He is the truth, He cannot lie.'" [6]

Thus the Christian people, echoing the words of the same St. Thomas, frequently sing the words:

"Sight, touch, and taste in Thee are each deceived, the ear alone most safely is believed. I believe all the Son of God has spoken — than truth's own word there is no truer token."

In fact, St. Bonaventure asserts: "There is no difficulty about Christ's presence in the Eucharist as in a sign, but that He is truly present in the Eucharist as He is in heaven, this is most difficult. Therefore to believe this is especially meritorious." [7]

Moreover, the Holy Gospel alludes to this when it tells of the many disciples of Christ who, after listening to the sermon about eating His Flesh and drinking His Blood, turned away and left our Lord, saying: "This is strange talk, who can be expected to listen to it?" Peter, on the other hand, in reply to Jesus' question whether also the twelve wished to leave, expressed his faith and that of the others promptly and resolutely with the marvelous answer: "Lord, to whom should we go? Thy words are the words of eternal life."[8]

It is logical, then, that we should follow as a guiding star in our investigations of this mystery the magisterium of the Church, to which the Divine Redeemer entrusted for protection and for explanation the revelation which He has communicated to us through Scripture or tradition. For we are convinced that "what since the days of antiquity was preached and believed throughout the whole Church with true Catholic Faith is true, even if it is not submitted to rational investigation, even if it is not explained by means of words."[9]

But this is not enough. Having safeguarded the integrity of the faith, it is necessary to safeguard also its proper mode of expression, lest by the careless use of words, we occasion (God forbid) the rise of false opinions regarding faith in the most sublime of mysteries. St. Augustine gives a stern warning about this in his consideration of the way of speaking employed by the philosophers of that which ought to be used by Christians.

"The philosophers," he says, "speak freely without fear of offending religious listeners on subjects quite difficult to understand. We, on the other hand, must speak according to a fixed norm, lest the lack of restraint in our speech result in some impious opinion even about the things signified by the words themselves." [10]

The Church, therefore, with the long labor of centuries, and, not without the help of the Holy Spirit, has established a rule of language and confirmed it with the authority of the councils. This rule, which has more than once been the watchword and banner of Orthodox faith, must be religiously preserved, and let no one presume to change it at his own pleasure or under the pretext of new science. Who would ever tolerate that the dogmatic formulas used by ecumenical councils for the mysteries of the Holy Trinity and the Incarnation be judged as no longer appropriate for men of our times and therefore that others be rashly substituted for them? In the same way it cannot be tolerated that any individual should on his own authority modify the formulas which were used by the Council of Trent to express belief in the Eucharistic Mystery. For these formulas, like the others which the Church uses to propose the dogmas of faith, express concepts which are not tied to a certain form of human culture, nor to a specific phase of human culture, nor to one or other theological school.

No, these formulas present that part of reality which necessary and universal experience permits the human mind to grasp and to manifest with apt and exact terms taken either from common or polished language. For this reason, these formulas are adapted to men of all times and all places. But the most sacred task of theology is, not the invention of new dogmatic formulas to replace old ones, but rather such a defense and explanation of the formulas adopted by the councils as may demonstrate that divine Revelation is the source of the truths communicated through these expressions.

It must be admitted that these formulas can sometimes be more clearly and accurately explained. In fact, the achievement of this goal is highly beneficial. But it would be wrong to give to these expressions a meaning other than the original. Thus the understanding of the faith should be advanced without threat to its unchangeable truth. It is, in fact, the teaching of the First Vatican Council that "the same signification (of sacred dogmas) is to be forever retained once our Holy Mother the Church has defined it, and under no pretext of deeper penetration may that meaning be weakened." [11]

THE MYSTERY OF THE EUCHARIST IS VERIFIED IN THE SACRIFICE OF THE MASS

For the inspiration and consolation of all, we wish to review with you, venerable brothers, the doctrine which the Catholic Church has always transmitted and unanimously teaches concerning the Mystery of the Eucharist.

We desire to recall at the very outset what may be termed the very essence of the dogma, namely, that by means of the Mystery of the Eucharist, the Sacrifice of the Cross, which was once offered on Calvary, is remarkably re-enacted and constantly recalled, and its saving power exerted for the forgiveness of those sins which we daily commit. [12]

Just as Moses with the blood of calves had sanctified the Old Testament, [13] so also Christ Our Lord, through the institution of the Mystery of the Eucharist, with His own Blood sanctified the New Testament, whose Mediator He is. For, as the Evangelists narrate, at the Last Supper "He took bread, and blessed and broke it, and gave it to them, saying: "This is My Body, given for you; do this for a commemoration of Me. And so with the cup, when supper was ended. This cup, he said, is the New Testament, in My Blood which is to be shed for you. [14] And by bidding the Apostles to do this in memory of Him, He made clear His will that the same sacrifice be forever repeated.

This intention of Christ was faithfully executed by the primitive Church through her adherence to the teaching of the Apostles and through her gatherings summoned to celebrate the Eucharistic Sacrifice. As St. Luke carefully testifies, "These occupied themselves continually with the Apostles' teaching, their fellowship in the breaking of bread, and the fixed times of prayer." [15] From this practice, the faithful used to derive such spiritual strength that it was said of them that "there was one heart and soul in all the company of believers."[16]

Moreover, the Apostle Paul, who has faithfully transmitted to us what he had received from the Lord, [17] is clearly speaking of the Eucharistic Sacrifice when he points out that Christians, precisely because they have been made partakers of the table of the Lord, ought not take part in pagan sacrifices. "Is not this cup we bless," he says, "a participation in Christ's Blood? Is not the Bread we break a participation in Christ's Body?. . . To drink the Lord's cup, and yet to drink the cup of evil spirits, to share the Lord's feast, and to share the feast of evil spirits, is impossible for you." [18] Foreshadowed by Malachias, [19] this new offering of the New Testament has always been offered by the Church, in accordance with the teaching of Our Lord and Apostles, "Not only to atone for the sins of the living faithful and to appeal for their other needs, but also to help these who have died in Christ but have not yet been completely purified." [20]

Passing over other citations, we recall merely the testimony rendered by St. Cyril of Jerusalem, who wrote the follow memorable instruction for his neophytes:

"After the Spiritual Sacrifice, the unbloody act of worship has been completed. Bending over this propitiatory offering we beg God to grant peace to all the Churches, to give harmony to the whole world, to bless our rulers, our soldiers, and our companions, to aid the sick and afflicted, and in general to assist all who stand in need; and then we offer the Victim also for our deceased holy ancestors and bishops for all our dead. As we do this, we are filled with the conviction that this Sacrifice will be of the greatest help to those souls for whom prayers are being offered in the very presence of our holy and awesome Victim."

This holy Doctor closes his instruction by citing the parallel of the crown which is woven for the emperor to move him to pardon exiles: "In the same fashion, when we offer our prayers to God for the dead, even though they be sinners, we weave no crown, but instead we offer Christ slaughtered for our sins, beseeching our merciful God to take pity both on them and on ourselves." [21]

St. Augustine testifies that this manner of offering also for the deceased "the Sacrifice which ransomed us" was being faithfully observed in the Church at Rome, [22] and at the same time he observes that the universal Church was following this custom in her conviction that it had been handed down by the earliest Fathers. [23]

To shed fuller light on the mystery of the Church, it helps to realize that it is nothing less than the whole Church which, in union with Christ in His role as Priest and Victim, offers the Sacrifice of the Mass and is offered in it. The Fathers of the Church taught this wondrous doctrine. [24] A few years ago our predecessor of happy memory, Pius XII, explained it, [25] and only recently the Second Vatican Council enunciated it in its treatise on the People of God as formulated in its Constitution on the Church. [26]

To be sure, the distinction between universal priesthood and hierarchical priesthood is one of essence and not merely one of degree, [27] and this distinction should be faithfully observed. Yet we cannot fail to be filled with the earnest desire that this teaching on the Mass be explained over and over until it takes root deep in the hearts of the faithful. Our desire is founded on our conviction that the correct understanding of the Eucharistic Mystery is the most effective means to foster devotion to this Sacrament, to extol the dignity of all the faithful, and to spur their spirit toward the attainment of the summit of sanctity, which is nothing less than the total offering of oneself to service of the Divine Majesty.

We should also mention "the public and social nature of every Mass," [28] a conclusion which clearly follows from the doctrine we have been discussing. For even though a priest should offer Mass in private, that Mass is not something private; it is an act of Christ and of the Church. In offering this Sacrifice, the Church learns to offer herself as a sacrifice for all. Moreover, for the salvation of the entire world she applies the single, boundless, redemptive power of the Sacrifice of the Cross. For every Mass is offered not for the salvation of ourselves alone, but also for that of the whole world.

Hence, although the very nature of the action renders most appropriate the active participation of many of the faithful in the celebration of the Mass, nevertheless, that Mass is to be fully approved which, in conformity with the prescriptions and lawful traditions of the Church, a priest for a sufficient reason offers in private, that is, in the presence of no one except his server. From such a Mass an abundant treasure of special salutary graces enriches the celebrant, the faithful, the whole Church, and the entire world — graces which are not imparted in the same abundance by the mere reception of Holy Communion.

Therefore, from a paternal and solicitous heart, we recommend to priests, who bestow on us a special crown of happiness in the Lord, that they be mindful of their power, received through the hands of the ordaining Bishop, of offering sacrifices to God and of celebrating Masses both for the living and for the dead in the name of the Lord, [29] and that they worthily and devoutly offer Mass each day in order that both they and the rest of the faithful may enjoy the benefits that flow so richly from the Sacrifice of the Cross. Thus also they will contribute most to the salvation of the human race.

IN THE SACRIFICE OF THE MASS CHRIST IS MADE SACRAMENTALLY PRESENT

By the few ideas which we have mentioned regarding the Sacrifice of the Mass, we are encouraged to explain a few notions concerning the Sacrament of the Eucharist, seeing that both sacrifice and Sacrament pertain inseparably to the same mystery. In an unbloody representation of the Sacrifice of the Cross and in application of its saving power, in the Sacrifice of the Mass the Lord is immolated when, through the words of consecration, He begins to be present in a sacramental form under the appearances of bread and wine to become the spiritual food of the faithful.

All of us realize that there is more than one way in which Christ is present in His Church. We wish to review at greater length the consoling doctrine which was briefly set forth in the constitution "De Sacra Liturgia." [30] Christ is present in His Church when she prays, since it is He who "prays for us and prays in us and to whom we pray as to our God." [31] It is He who has promised: "Where two or three are gathered together in My name, I am there in the midst of them." [32]

He is present in the Church as she performs her works of mercy, not only because we do to Christ whatever good we do to one of His least brethren, [33] but also because it is Christ, performing these works through the Church, who continually assists men with His divine love. He is present in the Church on her pilgrimage of struggle to reach the harbor of eternal life, since it is He who through faith dwells in our hearts [34] and, through the Holy Spirit whom He gives us, pours His love into those hearts. [35]

In still another genuine way He is present in the Church as she preaches, since the Gospel which he proclaims is the Word of God, which is not preached except in the name of Christ, by the authority of Christ, and with the assistance of Christ, the Incarnate Word of God. In this way there is formed "one flock which trusts its only shepherd." [36]

He is present in His Church as she governs the People of God, since her sacred power comes from Christ, and since Christ, "The Shepherd of Shepherds,"[37] is present in the pastors who exercise that power, according to His promise to the Apostles: "Behold I am with you all through the days that are coming, until the consummation of the world."

Moreover, in a manner still more sublime, Christ is present in His Church as she offers in His name the Sacrifice of the Mass; He is present in her as she administers the sacraments. We find deep consolation in recalling the accurate and eloquent words with which St. John Chrysostom, overcome with a sense of awe, described the presence of Christ in the offering of the Sacrifice of the Mass: "I wish to add something that is plainly awe-inspiring, but do not be astonished or upset. This Sacrifice, no matter who offers it, be it Peter or Paul, is always the same as that which Christ gave His disciples and which priests now offer: The offering of today is in no way inferior to that which Christ offered, because it is not men who sanctify the offering of today; it is the same Christ who sanctified His own. For just as the words which God spoke are the very same as those which the priest now speaks, so too the oblation is the very same." [38]

No one is unaware that the sacraments are the actions of Christ, who administers them through men. Therefore, the sacraments are holy in themselves, and by the power of Christ they pour grace into the soul when they touch the body. The mind boggles at these different ways in which Christ is present; they confront the Church with a mystery ever to be pondered.

But there is yet another manner in which Christ is present in His Church, a manner which surpasses all the others; it is His presence in the Sacrament of the Eucharist, which is for this reason "a more consoling source of devotion, a more lovely object of contemplation, a more effective means of sanctification than all the other sacraments." [39] The reason is clear; it contains Christ Himself and it is "a kind of perfection of the spiritual life; in a way, it is the goal of all the sacraments." [40]

This presence is called "real" — by which it is not intended to exclude all other types of presence as if they could not be "real" too, but because it is presence in the fullest sense: that is to say, it is a substantial presence by which Christ, the God-Man, is wholly and entirely present. [41] It would therefore be wrong to explain this presence by having recourse to the "spiritual" nature, as it is called, of the glorified Body of Christ, which is present everywhere, or by reducing it to a kind of symbolism, as if this most august Sacrament consisted of nothing else than an efficacious sign, "of the spiritual presence of Christ and of His intimate union with the faithful, members of His Mystical Body." [42]

It is true that much can be found in the Fathers and in the scholastics with regard to the symbolism of the Eucharist, especially with reference to the unity of the Church. The Council of Trent, restating their doctrine, taught that the Savior bequeathed the blessed Eucharist to His Church "as a symbol. . . of that unity and charity with which He wished all Christians to be most intimately united among themselves," and hence "as a symbol of that One Body of which He is the Head." [43]

When Christian literature was still in its infancy, the unknown author of that work we know as the "Didache or Teaching of the Twelve Apostles" wrote as follows on this subject: "In regard to the Eucharist, give thanks in this manner:. . . just as this bread was scattered and dispersed over the hills, but when harvested was made one, so may Your Church be gathered into Your kingdom from the ends of the earth." [44]

The same we read in St. Cyprian, writing in defense of the Church against schism: "Finally, the sacrifices of the Lord proclaim the unity of Christians, bound together by the bond of a firm and inviolable charity. For when the Lord, in speaking of bread which is produced by the compacting of many grains of wheat, refers to it as His Body, He is describing our people whose unity He has sustained, and when He refers to wine pressed from many grapes and berries, as His Blood, He is speaking of our flock, formed by the fusing of many united together." [45]

But before all of these, St. Paul had written to the Corinthians: the one bread makes us one body, though we are many in number the same bread is shared by all. [46]

While the eucharistic symbolism brings us to an understanding of the effect proper to this Sacrament, which is the unity of the mystical Body, it does not indicate or explain what it is that makes this Sacrament different from all others. The constant teaching which the Catholic Church passes on to her catechumens, the understanding of the Christian people, the doctrine defined by the Council of Trent, the very words used by Christ when He instituted the Most Holy Eucharist, compel us to acknowledge that "the Eucharist is that flesh of Our Savior Jesus Christ who suffered for our sins and whom the Father in His loving-kindness raised again." [47] To these words of St. Ignatius of Antioch, we may add those which Theodore of Mopsueta, a faithful witness to the faith of the Church at this point, addressed to the faithful: "The Lord did not say: This is a symbol of My Body, and this is a symbol of My blood but: This is My Body and My Blood." He teaches us not to look to the nature of those things which lie before us and are perceived by the senses, for by the prayer of thanksgiving and the words spoken over them, they have been changed into Flesh and Blood." [48]

The Council of Trent, basing itself on this faith of the Church, "openly and sincerely professes that within the Holy Sacrament of the Eucharist, after the Consecration of the bread and wine, Our Lord Jesus Christ, true God and true Man, really, truly and substantially contained under those outward appearances." In this way, the Savior in His humanity is present not only at the right hand of the Father according to the natural manner of existence, but also in the Sacrament of the Eucharist "by a mode of existence which we cannot express in words, but which, with a mind illumined by faith, we can conceive, and must most firmly believe, to be possible to God." [49]

CHRIST OUR LORD IS PRESENT IN THE SACRAMENT OF THE EUCHARIST BY TRANSUBSTANTIATION

To avoid misunderstanding this sacramental presence which surpasses the laws of nature and constitutes the greatest miracle of its kind [50] we must listen with docility to the voice of the teaching and praying Church. This voice, which constantly echoes the voice of Christ, assures us that the way Christ is made present in this Sacrament is none other than by the change of the whole substance of the bread into His Body, and of the whole substance of the wine into His Blood, and that this unique and truly wonderful change the Catholic Church rightly calls transubstantiation. [51] As a result of transubstantiation, the species of bread and wine undoubtedly take on a new meaning and a new finality, for they no longer remain ordinary bread and ordinary wine, but become the sign of something sacred, the sign of a spiritual food. However, the reason they take on this new significance and this new finality is simply because they contain a new "reality" which we may justly term ontological. Not that there lies under those species what was already there before, but something quite different; and that not only because of the faith of the Church, but in objective reality, since after the change of the substance or nature of the bread and wine into the Body and Blood of Christ, nothing remains of the bread and wine but the appearances under which Christ, whole and entire, in His physical "reality" is bodily present, although not in the same way that bodies are present in a given place.

For this reason the Fathers took special care to warn the faithful that in reflecting on this most august Sacrament, they should not trust to their senses, which reach only the properties of bread and wine, but rather to the words of Christ which have power to transform, change and transmute the bread and wine into His Body and Blood. For, as those same Fathers often said, the power that accomplishes this is that same power by which God Almighty, at the beginning of time, created the world out of nothing.

"We have been instructed in these matters and filled with an unshakable faith," says St. Cyril of Alexandria, at the end of a sermon on the mysteries of the faith, "that which seems to be bread, is not bread, though it tastes like it, but the Body of Christ, and that which seems to be wine, is not wine, though it too tastes as such, but the Blood of Christ. . . draw inner strength by receiving this bread as spiritual food and your soul will rejoice." [52]

St. John Chrysostom emphasizes this point, saying: "It is not the power of man which makes what is put before us the Body and Blood of Christ, but the power of Christ Himself who was crucified for us. The priest standing there in the place of Christ says these words but their power and grace are from God. 'This is My Body,' he says, and these words transform what lies before him." [53]

Cyril, Bishop of Alexandria, is in full agreement with the Bishop of Constantinople when he writes in his commentary on the Gospel of St. Matthew: "Christ said indicating (the bread and wine): 'This is My Body,' and 'This is My Blood,' in order that you might not judge what you see to be a mere figure. The offerings, by the hidden power of God Almighty, are changed into Christ's Body and Blood, and by receiving these we come to share in the life-giving and sanctifying efficacy of Christ." [54]

Ambrose, Bishop of Milan, dealing with the Eucharistic change, says: "Let us be assured that this is not what nature formed, but what the blessing consecrated, and that greater efficacy resides in the blessing than in nature, for by the blessing nature is changed." To confirm the truth of this mystery, he recounts many of the miracles described in the Scriptures, including Christ's birth of the Virgin Mary, and then turning to the work of creation, concludes thus: "Surely the word of Christ, which could make out of nothing that which did not exist, can change things already in existence into what they were not. For it is no less extraordinary to give things new natures than to change their natures." [55]

However, there is no need to assemble many testimonies. Rather let us recall that firmness of faith with which the Church with one accord opposed Berengarius, who, yielding to the difficulties of human reasoning, was the first who denied the Eucharistic change.

More than once she threatened to condemn him unless he retracted. Thus it was that our predecessor, St. Gregory VII, ordered him to pronounce the following oath:

> "I believe in my heart and openly profess that the bread and wine which are placed upon the altar are, by the mystery of the sacred prayer and the words of the Redeemer, substantially changed into the true and life-giving flesh and blood of Jesus Christ Our Lord, and that after the Consecration, there is present the true Body of Christ which was born of the Virgin and, offered up for the salvation of the world, hung on the Cross and now sits at the right hand of the Father, and that there is present the true Blood of Christ which flowed from His side. They are present not only by means of a sign and of the efficacy of the Sacrament, but also in the very reality and truth of their nature and substance." [56]

These words fully accord with the doctrine of the mystery of the Eucharistic change as set forth by the ecumenical councils. The constant teaching of these councils—of the Laterans of Constance, Florence and Trent,—whether stating the teaching of the Church or condemning errors, affords us an admirable example of the unchangingness of the Catholic Faith.

After the Council of Trent, our predecessor, Pius VI, on the occasion of the errors of the Synod of Pistia, warned parish priests when carrying out their office of teaching, not to neglect to speak of transubstantiation, one of the articles of faith. [57] Similarly our predecessor of happy memory, Pius XII, recalled the bounds which those who undertake to discuss the mystery of transubstantiation might not cross. [58] We our self also, in fulfillment of our apostolic office, have openly borne solemn witness to the faith of the Church at the National Eucharistic Congress held recently at Pisa. [59]

Moreover the Catholic Church has held on to this faith in the presence in the Eucharist of the Body and Blood of Christ, not only in her teaching but also in her practice, since she has at all times given to this great Sacrament the worship which is known as

Latria and which may be given to God alone. As St. Augustine says: "It was in His flesh that Christ walked among us and it is His flesh that He has given us to eat for our salvation. No one, however, eats of this without having first adored it... and not only do we not sin in thus adoring it, but we would sin if we did not do so."

LATREUTIC WORSHIP OF THE SACRAMENT OF THE EUCHARIST

The Catholic Church has always offered and still offers the cult of Latria to the Sacrament of the Eucharist, not only during Mass, but also outside of it, reserving Consecrated Hosts with the utmost care, exposing them to solemn veneration, and carrying them processionally to the joy of great crowds of the faithful.

In the ancient documents of the Church we have many testimonies of this veneration. The pastors of the Church in fact, solicitously exhorted the faithful to take the greatest care in keeping the Eucharist which they took to their homes. "The Body of Christ is meant to be eaten, not to be treated with irreverence," St. Hippolytus warns the faithful. [61]

In fact the faithful thought themselves guilty, and rightly so, as Origen recalls, if after they received the Body of the Lord in order to preserve it with all care and reverence, a small fragment of it fell off through negligence. [62]

The same pastors severely reproved those who showed lack of reverence if it happened. This is attested to by Novitianus whose testimony in the matter is trustworthy. He judged as deserving condemnation any one who came out of Sunday service carrying with him as usual the Eucharist, the sacred Body of the Lord, "not going to his house but running to places of amusement." [63]

On the other hand St. Cyril of Alexandria rejects as folly the opinion of those who maintained that if a part of the Eucharist was left over for the following day it did not confer sanctification. "For," he says, "neither Christ is altered nor His Holy Body changed, but the force and power and vivifying grace always remain with it." [64]

Nor should we forget that in ancient times the faithful, harassed by the violence of persecution or living in solitude out of love for monastic life nourished themselves even daily, receiving Holy Communion by their own hands when the priest or deacon was absent. [65]

We say this not in order that there may be some change in the way of keeping the Eucharist and of receiving Holy Communion which was later on prescribed by Church laws and which now remain in force, but rather that we may rejoice over the faith of the Church which is always one and the same.

This faith also gave rise to the feast of Corpus Christi which was first celebrated in the diocese of Liege specially through the efforts of the servant of God, Blessed Juliana of Mount Cornelius, and which our predecessor Urban IV extended to the Universal Church. From it have originated many practices of Eucharistic piety which under the inspiration of divine grace have increased from day to day and with which the Catholic Church is striving ever more to do homage to Christ, to thank Him for so great a gift and to implore His mercy.

EXHORTATION TO PROMOTE THE CULT OF THE EUCHARIST

We therefore ask you, venerable brothers, among the people entrusted to your care and vigilance, to preserve this faith in its purity and integrity — a faith which seeks only to remain perfectly loyal to the word of Christ and of the Apostles and unambiguously rejects all erroneous and mischievous opinions. Tirelessly promote the cult of the Eucharist, the focus where all other forms of piety must ultimately emerge.

May the faithful, thanks to your efforts, come to realize and experience ever more perfectly the truth of these words: "He who desires life finds here a place to live in and the means to live by. Let him approach, let him believe, let him be incorporated so that he may receive life. Let him not refuse union with the members, let him not be a corrupt member, deserving to be cut off, nor a disfigured member to be ashamed of. Let him be a grateful, fitting and healthy member. Let him cleave to the body, let him live by God and for God. Let him now labor here on earth, that he may afterwards reign in heaven." [66]

It is to be desired that the faithful, every day and in great numbers, actively participate in the Sacrifice of the Mass, receive Holy Communion with a pure heart, and give thanks to Christ our Lord for so great a gift. Let them remember these words: "The desire of Jesus Christ and of the Church that all the faithful receive daily Communion means above all that through the sacramental union with God they may obtain the strength necessary for mastering their passions, for purifying themselves of their daily venial faults and for avoiding the grave sins to which human frailty is exposed." [67]

In the course of the day the faithful should not omit to visit the Blessed Sacrament, which according to the liturgical laws must be kept in the churches with great reverence in a most honorable location. Such visits are a proof of gratitude, an expression of love, an acknowledgment of the Lord's presence.

No one can fail to understand that the Divine Eucharist bestows upon the Christian people an incomparable dignity. Not only while the sacrifice is offered and the sacrament is received, but as long as the Eucharist is kept in our churches and oratories, Christ is truly the Emmanuel, that is, "God with us." Day and night He is in our midst, he dwells with us, full of grace and truth. [68] He restores morality, nourishes virtues, consoles the afflicted, strengthens the weak. He proposes His own example to those who come to Him that all may learn to be, like Himself, meek and humble of heart and to seek not their own interests but those of God.

Anyone who approaches this august Sacrament with special devotion and endeavors to return generous love for Christ's own infinite love, will experience and fully understand—not without spiritual joy and fruit—how precious is the life hidden with Christ in God [69] and how great is the value of converse with Christ, for there is nothing more consoling on earth, nothing more efficacious for advancing along the road of holiness.

Further, you realize, venerable brothers, that the Eucharist is reserved in the churches and oratories as in the spiritual center of a religious community or of a parish, yes, of the universal Church and of all of humanity, since beneath the appearance of the species, Christ is contained, the invisible Head of the Church, the Redeemer of the World, the Center of all hearts, "by whom all things are and by whom we exist." [70]

From this it follows that the worship paid to the Divine Eucharist strongly impels the soul to cultivate a "social" love, [71] by which the common good is given preference over the good of the individual. Let us consider as our own the interests of the community, of the parish, of the entire Church, extending our charity to the whole world, because we know that everywhere there are members of Christ.

The Eucharistic Sacrament, venerable brothers, is the sign and the cause of the unity of the Mystical Body, and it inspires an active "ecclesial" spirit in those who venerate it with great fervor. Therefore, never cease to persuade those committed to your care that they should learn to make their own the cause of the Church, in approaching the eucharistic mystery to pray to God without interruption to offer themselves to God as a pleasing sacrifice for the peace and unity of the Church, so that all the children of the Church be united and think the same, that there be no divisions among them, but rather unity of mind and purpose, as the Apostles insist. [72] May all those not yet in perfect communion with the Catholic Church, who though separated from her glory in the name of Christian, share with us as soon as possible with the help of divine grace that unity of faith and communion which Christ wanted to be the distinctive mark of His disciples.

This zeal in praying and consecrating one's self to God for the unity of the Church should be practiced particularly by religious, both men and women, inasmuch as they are in a special way devoted to the adoration of the Blessed Sacrament, according it homage and honor on earth, in virtue of their vows.

Nothing has ever been or is more important to the Church or more consoling than the desire for the unity of all Christians, a desire which we wish to express once again in the very words used by the Council of Trent at the close of its decree on the Most Blessed Eucharist: "In conclusion, the sacred synod with paternal love admonishes, exhorts, prays and implores 'through the merciful kindness of our God' [73] that each and every Christian come at last to a perfect agreement regarding this sign of unity, this bond of charity, this symbol of concord, and, mindful of such great dignity and such exquisite love of Christ Our Lord who gave His beloved soul as the price of our salvation and 'his flesh to eat' [74] believe and adore these sacred mysteries of His Body and Blood with such firm and unwavering faith, with such devotion, piety and veneration, that they can receive frequently that super-substantial bread, [75] which will be for them truly the life of the soul and unfailing strength of mind, so that fortified by its vigor [76] they can depart from this wretched pilgrimage on earth to reach their heavenly home where they will then eat the same 'bread of angels' [77] no longer hidden by the species which now they eat under the sacred appearances." [78]

May the all-good Redeemer who shortly before His death prayed to the Father that all who were to believe in Him would be one even as He and the Father were one [79] deign speedily to hear our most ardent prayer and that of the entire Church, that we may all with one voice and one faith, celebrate the Eucharistic Mystery and, by participating in the Body of Christ, become one body, [80] linked by those same bonds which He Himself desire for its perfection.

And we turn with paternal affection also to those who belong to the venerable Churches of the Orient, from which came so many most illustrious Fathers whose testimony to the belief of the Eucharist we have so gladly cited in our present letter. Our soul is filled with intense joy as we consider your faith in the Eucharist, which is also our faith, and as we listen to the liturgical prayers by which you celebrate so great a mystery we rejoice to behold your eucharistic devotion, and to read your theologians explaining or defending the doctrine of this most august Sacrament.

May the Most Blessed Virgin Mary from whom Christ Our Lord took the flesh which under the species of bread and wine "is contained, offered and consumed," [81] may all the saints of God, specially those who burned with a more ardent devotion to the Divine Eucharist, intercede before the Father of mercies so that from this same faith in and devotion toward the Eucharist may result and flourish a perfect unity of communion among all Christians.

Unforgettable are the words of the holy martyr Ignatius, in his warning to the faithful of Philadelphia against the evils of division and schism, the remedy for which lies in the Eucharist: "Strive then," he said, "to make use of one form of thanksgiving for the flesh of Our Lord Jesus Christ is one and one is the chalice in the union of His Blood, one altar, one bishop." [82]

Encouraged by the most consoling hope of the blessings which will accrue to the whole Church and the entire world from an increase in devotion to the Eucharist, with profound affection we impart to you, venerable brothers, to the priests, Religious and all those who collaborate with you and to all the faithful entrusted in your care, the apostolic benediction as a pledge of heavenly graces.

Given at Rome, at St. Peter's, the third day of September, the Feast of St. Pius X, in the year 1965, the third year of our pontificate.

> Paul VI, Pope
> (footnotes omitted)

Chapter Seven

The Code of Canon Law

In this Chapter that part of Canon Law that pertains to the Most Holy Eucharist will be cited.

TITLE III: THE MOST HOLY EUCHARIST

Can. 897 The most venerable Sacrament is the Most Holy Eucharist, in which Christ the Lord Himself is contained, offered and received, and by which the Church continually lives and grows. The Eucharistic Sacrifice, the memorial of the death and resurrection of the Lord, in which the Sacrifice of the cross is forever perpetuated, is the summit and the source of all worship and Christian life. By means of it the unity of God's people is signified and brought about, and the building up of the body of Christ is perfected. The other Sacraments and all the apostolic works of Christ are bound up with, and directed to, the Most Holy Eucharist.

Can. 898 Christ's faithful are to hold the Most Holy Eucharist in the highest honor. They should take an active part in the celebration of the most august Sacrifice of the Mass; they should receive the Sacrament with great devotion and frequently, and should reverence It with the greatest adoration. In explaining the doctrine of this Sacrament, pastors of souls are assiduously to instruct the faithful about their obligation in this regard.

Chapter 1

THE CELEBRATION OF THE EUCHARIST

Can. 899 #1 The celebration of the Eucharist is an action of Christ Himself and of the Church. In it Christ the Lord, through the ministry of the Priest, offers Himself, substantially present under the appearance of bread and wine, to God the Father, and gives Himself as spiritual nourishment to the faithful who are associated with Him in His offering. #2 In the Eucharistic assembly the people of God are called together under the presidency of the Bishop or of a Priest authorized by him, who act in the person of Christ. All the faithful present, whether clerics or lay people, unite and participate in their own way, according to their various orders and liturgical roles. #3 The Eucharistic celebration is to be so ordered that all the participants derive from it the many fruits for which Christ the Lord instituted the Eucharistic Sacrifice.

Article 1: The Minister of the Most Holy Eucharist

Can. 900 #1 The only minister who, in the person of Christ, can bring into being the Sacrament of the Eucharist, is a validly ordained Priest. #2 Any priest who is not debarred by canon law may lawfully celebrate the Eucharist, provided the provisions of the following canons are observed.

Can. 901 A Priest entitled to offer Mass for anyone, living or dead.

Can. 902 Priest may concelebrate the Eucharist unless the welfare of the Christian faithful requires or urges otherwise but with due regard for the freedom of each priest to celebrate the Eucharist individually, though not during the time when there is a celebration in the same church or oratory.

Can. 903 A Priest is to be permitted to celebrate the Eucharist, even if he is not known to the Rector of the church, provided either that he presents commendatory letters, not more than a year old, from his own Ordinary or Superior, or that it can be prudently judged that he is not debarred from celebrating.

Can. 904 Remembering always that in the mystery of the Eucharistic Sacrifice the work of redemption is continually being carried out, Priests are to celebrate frequently. Indeed, daily celebration is earnestly recommended, because, even if it should not be possible to have the faithful present, it is an action of Christ and of the Church in which Priests fulfil their principal role.

Can. 905 #1 Apart from those cases in which the law allows him to celebrate or concelebrate the Eucharist a number of times on the same day, a Priest may not celebrate more than once a day. #2 If there is a scarcity of Priests, the local Ordinary may for a good reason allow Priests to celebrate twice in one day or even, if Pastoral need requires it, three times on Sundays or Holy Days of

Obligation.

Can. 906 A Priest may not celebrate the Eucharistic Sacrifice without the participation of at least one of the faithful, unless there is a good and reasonable cause for doing so.

Can. 907 In the celebration of the Eucharist, deacons and lay persons are not permitted to say the prayers, especially the Eucharistic prayer, nor to perform the actions which are proper to the celebrating Priest.

Can. 908 Catholic Priests are forbidden to concelebrate the Eucharist with priests or ministers of churches or ecclesial communities which are not in full communion with the Catholic Church.

Can. 909 A Priest is not to omit dutifully to prepare himself by prayer before the celebration of the Eucharist, nor afterwards to omit to make thanksgiving to God.

Can. 910 #1 The ordinary Minister of Holy Communion is a Bishop, a Priest or a Deacon. #2 The extraordinary minister of Holy Communion is an acolyte, or another of Christ's faithful deputed in accordance with Can. 230 #3.

Can. 911 #1 The duty and right to bring the Holy Eucharist to the sick as Viaticus belongs to the parish Priest, to assistant Priests, to Chaplains and, in respect of all who are in the house, to the community Superior in clerical religious institutes or societies of apostolic life. #2 In a case of necessity, or with the permission at least presumed of the parish Priest, Chaplain or Superior, who must subsequently be notified, any Priest or other minister of Holy Communion must do this.

Article 2: Participation in The Most Holy Eucharist

Can. 912 Any baptized person who is not forbidden by law may and must be admitted to Holy Communion.

Can. 913 #1 For Holy Communion to be administered to children, it is required that they have sufficient knowledge and be accurately prepared, so that according to their capacity they understand what the mystery of Christ means, and are able to receive the Body of the Lord with faith and devotion. #2 The Holy Eucharist may, however, be administered to children in danger of death if they can distinguish the Body of Christ from ordinary food and receive Communion with reverence.

Can. 914 It is primarily the duty of parents and of those who take their place, as it is the duty of the parish priest, to ensure that children who have reached the use of reason are properly prepared and, having made their sacramental confession, are nourished by this divine food as soon as possible. It is also the duty of the parish priest to see that children who have not reached the use of reason, or whom he has judged to be insufficiently disposed, do not come to Holy Communion.

Can. 915 Those upon whom the penalty of excommunication or interdict has been imposed or declared, and others who obstinately persist in manifest grave sin, are not to be admitted to Holy Communion.

Can. 916 Anyone who is conscious of grave sin may not celebrate Mass or receive the Body of the Lord without previously having been to sacramental Confession, unless there is a grave reason and there is no opportunity to confess; in this case the person is to remember the obligation to make an act of perfect contrition, which includes the resolve to go to confession as soon as possible.

Can. 917 One who has received the Holy Eucharist may receive it again on the same day only within a Eucharistic celebration in which that person participates, without prejudice to the provision of Can. 921 #2.

Can. 918 It is most strongly recommended that the faithful receive Holy Communion in the course of a Eucharistic celebration. If, however, for good reason they ask for It apart from the Mass, it is to be administered to them, observing the liturgical rites.

Can. 919 #1 Whoever is to receive the Holy Eucharist is to abstain for at least one hour before Holy Communion from all food and drink, with the sole exception of water and medicine. #2 A priest who, on the same day, celebrates the Holy Eucharist twice or three times may consume something before the second or third celebration, even though there is not an hour's interval. #3 The elderly and those who are suffering from some illness, as well as those who care for them, may receive the Holy Eucharist even if within the preceding hour they have consumed something.

Can. 920 #1 Once admitted to the Most Holy Eucharist, each of the faithful is obliged to receive Holy Communion at least once a year. #2 This precept must be fulfilled during paschal time, unless for a good reason it is fulfilled at another time during the year.

Can. 921 #1 Christ's faithful who are in danger of death, from whatever cause, are to be strengthened by Holy Communion as Viaticus. #2 Even if they have already received Holy Communion that same day, it is nevertheless strongly suggested that in danger of death they should communicate again. #3 While the danger of death persists, it is recommended that Holy Communion be administered a number of times, but on separate days.

Can. 922 Holy Viaticus for the sick is not to be unduly delayed. Those who have the care of souls are to take assiduous care that the sick are strengthened by It while they are in full possession of their faculties.

Can. 923 Christ's faithful may participate in the Eucharistic Sacrifice and receive Holy Communion in any Catholic rite, without prejudice to the provisions of Can. 844.

Article 3: The Rites and Ceremonies of the Eucharistic Celebration

Can. 924 §1 The most holy Sacrifice of the Eucharist must be celebrated in bread, and in wine to which a small quantity of water is to be added. §2 The bread must be wheaten only, and recently made, so that there is no danger of corruption. §3 The wine must be natural, made from grapes of the vine, and not corrupt.

Can. 925 Holy communion is to be given under the species of bread alone or, in accordance with the liturgical laws, under both species or, in case of necessity, even under the species of wine alone.

Can. 926 In the eucharistic celebration, in accordance with the ancient tradition of the Latin Church, the priest is to use unleavened bread wherever he celebrates Mass.

Can. 927 It is absolutely wrong, even in urgent and extreme necessity, to consecrate one element without the other, or even to consecrate both outside the eucharistic celebration.

Can. 928 The eucharistic celebration is to be carried out either in the Latin language or in another language, provided the liturgical texts have been lawfully approved.

Can. 929 In celebrating and administering the Eucharist, priests and deacons are to wear the sacred vestments prescribed by the rubrics.

Can. 930 §1 A priest who is ill or elderly, if he is unable to stand, may celebrate the eucharistic Sacrifice sitting but otherwise observing the liturgical laws; he may not, however, do so in public except by permission of the local Ordinary. §2 A priest who is blind or suffering from some other infirmity, may lawfully celebrate the eucharistic Sacrifice by using the text of any approved Mass, with the assistance, if need be, of another priest or deacon or even a properly instructed lay person.

Article 4: The Time and Place of the Eucharistic Celebration

Can. 931 The celebration and distribution of the Eucharist may take place on any day and at any hour, except those which are excluded by the liturgical laws.

Can. 932 §1 The eucharistic celebration is to be carried out in a sacred place, unless in a particular case necessity requires otherwise; in which case the celebration must be in a fitting place. §2 The eucharistic Sacrifice must be carried out at an altar that is dedicated or blessed. Outside a sacred place an appropriate table may be used, but always with an altar cloth and a corporal.

Can. 933 For a good reason, with the express permission of the local Ordinary and provided scandal has been eliminated, a priest may celebrate the Eucharist in a place of worship of any Church or ecclesial community which is not in full communion with the catholic Church.

CHAPTER II : THE RESERVATION AND VENERATION OF THE MOST HOLY EUCHARIST

Can. 934 §1 The Most Holy Eucharist:

1. must be reserved in the cathedral church or its equivalent, in every parish church and in the church or oratory attached to the house of a religious institute or society of apostolic life;

2. may be reserved in the chapel of a bishop and, with the permission of the local ordinary, in other churches, oratories and chapels.

§2 In sacred places where the Most Holy Eucharist is reserved there must always be someone who is responsible for it, and as far as possible a priest is to celebrate Mass there at least twice a month.

Can. 935 It is not lawful for anyone to keep the Most Holy Eucharist in personal custody or to carry it around, unless there is an urgent pastoral need and the prescriptions of the diocesan Bishop are observed.

Can. 936 In a house of a religious institute or other house of piety, the Most Holy Eucharist is to be reserved only in the church or principal oratory attached to the house. For a just reason, however, the Ordinary can permit it to be reserved also in another oratory of the same house.

Can. 937 Unless there is a grave reason to the contrary, a church in which the Most Holy Eucharist is reserved is to be open to the faithful for at least some hours every day, so that they can pray before the blessed Sacrament.

Can. 938 §1 The Most Holy Eucharist is to be reserved habitually in only one tabernacle of a church or oratory. §2 The tabernacle in which the Most Holy Eucharist is reserved should be sited in a distinguished place in the church or oratory, a place which is conspicuous, suitably adorned and conducive to prayer. §3 The tabernacle in which the Most Holy Eucharist is habitually reserved is to be immovable, made of solid and non-transparent material, and so locked as to give the greatest security against any danger of profanation. §4 For a grave reason, especially at night, it is permitted to reserve the Most Holy Eucharist in some other safer place, provided it is fitting. §5 The person in charge of a church or oratory is to see to it that the key of the tabernacle in which the Most Holy Eucharist is reserved, is in maximum safe keeping.

Can. 939 Consecrated hosts, in a quantity sufficient for the needs of the faithful, are to be kept in a pyx or ciborium, and are to be renewed frequently, the older hosts having been duly consumed.

Can. 940 A special lamp is to burn continuously before the

tabernacle in which the Most Holy Eucharist is reserved, to indicate and to honor the presence of Christ.

Can. 941 §1 In churches or oratories which are allowed to reserve the Most Holy Eucharist, there may be exposition, either with the pyx or with the monstrance, in accordance with the norms prescribed in the liturgical books. §2 Exposition of the blessed Sacrament may not take place while Mass is being celebrated in the same area of the church or oratory.

Can. 942 It is recommended that in these churches or oratories, there is to be each year a solemn exposition of the blessed Sacrament for an appropriate, even if not for a continuous time, so that the local community may more attentively meditate on and adore the eucharistic mystery. This exposition is to take place only if a fitting attendance of the faithful is foreseen, and the prescribed norms are observed.

Can. 943 The minister of exposition of the blessed Sacrament and of the eucharistic blessing is a priest or deacon. In special circumstances the minister of exposition and deposition alone, but without the blessing, is an acolyte, and extraordinary minister of holy communion, or another person deputed by the local Ordinary, in accordance with the regulations of the diocesan Bishop.

Can. 944 §1 Wherever in the judgement of the diocesan Bishop it can be done, a procession through the streets is to be held, especially on the solemnity of the Body and Blood of Christ, as a public witness of veneration of the Most Holy Eucharist. §2 It is for the diocesan Bishop to establish such regulations about processions as will provide for participation in them and for their being carried out in a dignified manner.

Chapter Eight

Conclusion and Consolation For The Loyal Catholic In Today's Church

Catholics today pray the same creed the world over, yet in the United States many feel that there are at least two bodies of believers that consider themselves to make up the one and true Holy, Catholic, and Apostolic Church; each body claiming to be the real Mystical Body of Christ.

We know that Jesus spoke of only one Church; He founded only one Church, one body that was to function on earth in His name, and He would be the Head of this Mystical Body of Christ. There can be only one truth, and it is Jesus. There can be only one Head, and it is Jesus. There can be only one Mystical Body of Christ and that body is made up of the Church believers who are loyal to the Pope and the bishops who are loyal to him. And together the Pope and those loyal bishops are the authentic Magisterium, the true teaching authority of the Church on earth.

If there is more than one body claiming to be His Mystical Body on earth then there exists a monumental dilemma for those members whose faith is built on sand and not built on the foundation which is the Magisterium. They are vulnerable to hearing and believing all kinds of deviations from the truth which is held only by the authentic Magisterium

It is my sincere belief that those Catholics who will remain loyal to the Magisterium through hailstorm of controversy and error that faces the church in this new millennium will actually be part of the remnant faithful who will help preserve the Roman Catholic Church on this earth. It will not be a cakewalk for them. Suffering is the name of the game for any spiritual victory as shown in the lives of the saints and martyrs, but especially in the lives of Jesus, Mary, and St. Joseph when they walked this earth.

In referring once again to the mind-boggling statistics of the handful of Catholics that believe in the Real Presence (approximately 30 percent), and the 3 percent that frequent the Sacrament of Reconciliation, we are faced with the heart-breaking story of the Catholic situation in the United States. It is even worse in the so-called Catholic countries in Europe. Short of a real miracle of grace from God Himself, there is little reason to hope that this situation will change anytime soon. In short, the authentic Roman Catholic believer needs to recognize that, perhaps for the first time in their Catholic lives, they have a veritable cross to bear and possibly for the rest of their earthly existence. What indications are there coming from the National Council of Catholic Bishops that we will soon return to a unified Catholic Church and that the liturgists have been brought under some control, and the seminaries are under strict surveillance, and the progressive bishops and clergy are being disciplined by the hierarchy here or in Rome?

MANY CHANGES

Since Vatican Council II Catholics have seen substantial change in the liturgy, the most obvious being the departure from the Tridentine Latin Mass. Gregorian Chant has practically disappeared from Mass, even in monasteries. It is known for a fact that more than one priest celebrated Mass while wearing a clown suit. The most serious cases of liturgical abuse concern the question as to whether or not the Mass is valid and do the people really receive a properly consecrated host.

There is really no need to itemize the various abuses and deviations from approved rubrics. Those who are reading this book have their own catalog of questionable or invalid liturgical practices. The point of this book is to emphasize that things are unlikely to change and they might even get worse before they get better. Living with these conditions for many will not be easy. Changing parishes or dioceses is not always possible and the Catholic who must live with such an unhappy situation is indeed being put to the test.

The apparent lack of sameness is hard for many to take. The differences between parishes and dioceses cause confusion and instability within the Church. The security found in One Mother Church and the consistency of practices throughout the Church which we once knew and loved is simply gone and perhaps gone forever.

TWO BLOCKS

The two Churches that seem to be functioning in the United States have their foundation in how the bishops, priests, religious, and laity view the obligation to be loyal to the Magisterium; to be loyal to or independent from the Magisterium.

In the one Church of traditional Catholics the members are loyal to and supportive of the Pope and those bishops in union with him in all aspects of the dogmas and doctrines, and traditions. They feel it is a sacred duty to be obedient to this traditional Church. On the other hand we have the Catholics who believe THEY are the true Catholics and it is their duty to object and to change "the old-fashioned" ways of the Church. They tend to disagree with the Pope and his loyal bishops on major facets of the faith. The predicament of the laity is truly painful, confusing, and seemingly hopeless.

It seems that the attempt at democratization of the Church has led to disobedience. Those religious orders that want to vote on every issue or rebel against authority with whom there is disagreement reject the flow of authority from above. It also seems that there is a widespread breakdown of discipline at all levels of Church officialdom. Some bishops flex their ecclesiastical muscles in apparent disregard of the Vatican position in serious matters. Some priests are very progressive when their bishop is conservative, and the reverse is true as well.

The laity generally does not have a sufficient knowledge or understanding of the scope of authority granted to bishops and cardinals. They are not able to judge the parameters within which the hierarchy may operate without violating Church law in the area of liturgy and various Church practices. The laity does not know when the bishop may deviate from the General Instructions of the Roman Missal. In a certain major diocese in the United States some of the loyal Catholics are completely confounded over the changes imposed on them, and according to them, without any rational reasons. High-handed actions concerning architectural changes to church buildings, and placement of the tabernacle, and when the congregation kneels or stands, or how they process to Holy Communion, and many other changes from what was considered satisfactory in the past, are very upsetting to Catholics who desperately want to hold on to what is dear to them and provides for them a tie to the one true Catholic Church. Perhaps the education of the people of God by a thoughtful and patient leader rather than a dictatorial attitude towards those who pay the bills, could overcome the anxieties. Many feel disenfranchised by their own Church. They are confused, hurt, and angry because of such an approach by their bishop and they feel that most changes enforced upon them are disruptive and destructive to the unity of the diocese. Most of us do not know the limits of the bishops' authority. Not knowing can lead to suspicions of motives.

The loyal catholics want to be "good" Catholics and want to be able to love and obey their bishop. They are torn between obedience to him and obedience to the Magisterium if they see him acting out of concert with the Magisterium. This dilemma applies also to hundreds of priests and religious who feel the same way about their bishop. And the priest is totally dependent upon his bishop for his financial health and retirement. The threat of loss of an earned retirement is a very serious threat indeed and so what does the "good" priest do when he is not of the progressive or modernist mold?

What a pitiful state the Church has come to for those who have given their lives to the Church as clergy or as lay people. They want to serve and participate as members of the authentic Catholic Church. But should we be surprised by the confusion and open conflicts, especially those that exist between loyal bishops and many so-called theologians? Should we wonder how the Church can grow in strength when the presidents of Catholic colleges and universities are so headstrong in opposing Rome and asserting their "academic freedom" in their teaching and actions which are in conflict with Rome?

Why should anyone be surprised at the state of things? Pope Paul VI said that " the smoke of Satan" has entered into the sanctuary. Pope Leo XIII said that in a vision he saw God, the Father, give Lucifer a span of one hundred years, during which he will have unusual powers to attempt to destroy the Church. No, we should not be surprised but rather we should have been enlightened years ago to recognize that the tribulation and the purification would come and try us all. No matter the sincerity of the motives of the bishops of the Church; no matter their sincere intentions. They are susceptible to temptations and suggestions by Satan who can use all of us by misleading us through his suggestions and inspirations, making us do wrong when we think we are doing good. This is precisely why it is a major necessity for us to pray for priests and bishops as requested by Our Lady at Fatima and Akita. The resultant confusion and disruption, the demoralization of clergy and laity; the tearing down and ripping apart of the unity which was once the hallmark of this Catholic Church, can be attributed to Satan and those who are susceptible to his plans to destroy this Church.

The speedy downward spiral of the effectiveness and breakup of the unity of this Church during the past 30 years or so can be attributed to the work of Evil. Confusion and disunity are evidence of Satan's hand in the Church today. The third secret of Fatima as revealed to the public by Cardinal Ratzinger in the year 2000, clearly describes the persecution and terrorization of the Popes and the Church over the past 100 years. Apparently this suffering of the Church is still part of our immediate future but now it involves the laity to a much greater extent than it did before Vatican Council II.

The Church, as the Mystical Body of Christ on earth, is suffering her own special climb up Golgotha and is experiencing a kind of purification, which includes the clergy and the laity. This Mystical Body of Christ will pass through its own crucible of pain and suffering before its resurrection into a new springtime. This leads us to the conclusion that each Catholic who considers himself or herself to be loyal to the authentic one and holy Catholic Church, should see themselves as members of the Remnant and destined to carry a cross uniquely tailored to each one, into the unknown future.

It is required of us to be obedient to whatever legally appointed Church authority to whom we are responsible. Although we are never obligated to obey any order or request that is against Faith and Morals, we are required to otherwise be obedient even when there can be serious disagreements and personal upset. In those cases we are to pray "without ceasing" and for those who can, we are to fast because there is a cost to any spiritual victory. Our Church teaches that nothing happens that God does not either directly cause or permit to happen... nothing. The bible teaches that He can bring forth good from what appears to be evil if we have but faith and believe in Him. It seems God has permitted this current dilemma in the Church and has done so for His reasons. His ways are not our ways. We must trust in Him.

For those who will be members of the "Remnant," which by its very name implies that there will be relatively few in this select group which will remain loyal to Christ and His Church—those few will be required to carry a cross of considerable weight in the form of obedience to the legally constituted Church. We know all forms of suffering can and should be offered to God, and through such suffering we can contribute to the resurrection of this Church and the re-establishment of its glory for the coming triumph of the Immaculate Heart of Mary. This remnant will be the means of pre-serving the Catholic Church as it was founded by Jesus Christ but it will be through prayer, suffering, and fasting. Jesus told us clearly that some evil spirits can be removed only through prayer with fasting! The loyal Catholic has a job to do! Be grateful for the great privilege you have received from Jesus Christ. You are called to be a member of His Remnant.

Whatever we wish to label them, it seems that the reality of the Church in the United States is that two blocks exist; one is made up of the Catholics who believe in and support and obey the Magisterium, the AUTHENTIC Magisterium, i.e. the Holy Father and those bishops in union with him; the other Church, which many say is now the American Catholic Church, is made up of those progressive Catholics who want to modernize the "old Church's" teachings and they could not care less about what the Holy Father has to say. Within this "American Catholic Church" is a vast range of beliefs, ranging from New Age and Modernism to the nominal Catholic who knows little about the Faith and bends with the wind ... that is, they pick and choose what suits them and usually follow the trendy "stuff" so long as it is not of the traditional beliefs.

Canon Law and the GIRM

If violators of Canon Law are not taken to task or never disciplined, it really doesn't matter what the General Instruction of the Roman Missal (GIRM) requires for compliance. If a bishop or cardinal has what amounts to unlimited authority to circumvent the GIRM because of local circumstances then we can expect unlimited variations from the GIRM among the various dioceses. The GIRM should be complied with by all authorities.

Pride Might Be A Factor

Caution should be given great consideration before complaints grow into open rebellion over disagreements and deviations from the GIRM. One basic question should be asked of ourselves when tempted to complain to the pastor or bishop: has this or that "new change" which we question, in any way curtailed or interfered with those graces we would expect before the change? Have the spiritual benefits of Mass been diminished in any way?

Or are we discontented because we have a personal preference for things the way they used to be and now someone has stepped on our pride and our feelings? Is it really God's will we want to satisfy or is it our will that gets the priority? Are we waging our own personal spiritual warfare with our spiritual superiors who are duly appointed by the Church, for inconsequential reasons for the sake of one-upmanship and an assertion of our personal power in the community? We all know why God loves the simple and the humble. We ourselves gravitate to such people in our social circles because they aren't always challenging those with whom they feel superior. Pride really is the root of all evil and heaven forbid that any of us falsely justify our rebellion against official authority because we are so filled with ourselves that there is no room left for God's will and a holy obedience in our own life.

Difficult Times

There is no question as to the painful nature of our seeing "changes that make no sense" or that cause inconvenience, or change the status quo and disturb our inner peace. But these are not normal times in the Church. The turmoil is very real and destructive, but it is also cleansing, purifying, and instructive if we live in the will of God.

Not all changes imposed through the liturgy can be blamed on Evil. We must do a thorough examination of our own motives before we register complaints to the priest or bishop and before we allow it to disturb our peace. Remembering that God causes or permits everything that happens can be a powerful restraining force on our tempers and actions. Taking the time to give due consideration to the motives of the bishop and trying to see his side of the "problem," in other words," walking in his moccasins," might allow us to see the good in certain changes and not fault him with wrong motives. We need to credit him with enough wisdom to know that no matter how "progressive" or disrupting his policies might be, he is intelligent enough to know he will answer to God one day for every action taken as a shepherd of the Church. Obedience is a virtue and leads to the kind of peace that only God can provide. It strengthens our will against pride and is therefore beautiful and redeeming in the eyes of God.

Prime Concern

Our prime concern is whether or not the mass we attend is a valid Mass and did we receive the Body, Blood, Soul, and Divinity of Our Lord? As Christians we have a paramount responsibility to demonstrate good will to all, especially our religious superiors. If any doubt exists concerning Mass and the Holy Eucharist one should have the courage and courtesy to speak with the pastor or to their spiritual advisor, and to bring up the matter in a peaceful and intelligent manner. So prayer is important as a part of the approach to finding out what one needs to know to clarify things. With prayer as a prelude to approaching the pastor or bishop, one can satisfy oneself that he or she is really acting in good faith and as Jesus would in a similar situation. It is a sign of Christian charity in action to ask oneself how would Jesus act in this situation? The answer always is: He would act with kindness, love, and try hard to give the benefit of the doubt to the other party and judge the motives in a positive light if possible. We need to remember that we receive mercy from Him only when we give mercy.

Losing our peace in any such conflict with the pastor or bishop is not a positive sign at all. It is almost always a sign that pride is at work and the devil is sitting on our shoulder, calling the shots, so to speak, and using us as his tool. Losing our peace is a sign that we are on our way to becoming part of the problem instead of part of the solution.

As a marriage and family counselor, I can testify to this fact—pride is the greatest impediment to finding solutions to family and marital problems. Jesus doesn't "hang around" too long when humility has left the scene. Self-seeking and every form of pride is the death knell for progress in solving any problem.

Spiritual Weapons For Spiritual Warfare

It might seem like an over-simplification to say that prayer and fasting does more than our feeble human efforts in spiritual warfare. It is a waste of time to convince one who has no genuine prayer life. How would they even measure any success based on prayer or fasting if these are strangers to their lifestyle? Jesus does not give false hope or erroneous advice. The gospel tells us to pray always for Satan is lurking everywhere to trip us up and cause our downfall. No one is immune to his efforts and we are but weaklings compared to his intelligence and powers. Prayer and fasting are the real antidotes to his power and cunning. Being in the state of grace has to be a top priority for us. Many do not reason that good works gain no heavenly merit if one is not in the state of grace. Aside from the risk of dying in such a state and going to Hell for eternity, it makes spiritual common sense to remain friends with God if we need His supernatural help (grace) to fight the battles of spiritual warfare. The daily examination of conscience and reflection on our own motives and actions are very helpful in preventing our fooling ourselves as we leap into the fray with no armaments to shield us and overlooking the pride that might be at work.

Motives of the Shepherds

No one is immune to the Evil One's power of suggestion. Remember what happened to St. Peter in the aftermath of Jesus' suffering in the garden? The first vicar of Christ on earth gave in to cowardice and denied Christ three times. Why would we think that our present day shepherds, the bishops, would not succumb to the possibility of being misled with erroneous suggestions by Satan. It is possible that some of them impose strange requests because they really believe they are doing good when in fact they are doing wrong. What was it that St. Paul said about not doing that which he wants to do but rather doing that which he wants at all costs to avoid doing? This is the great St. Paul who admits to the power of temptation. Let's remember that Jesus is permitting these things to happen for His own purposes. The apostles were weak and we can expect no more from our bishops with their human limitations. And these bishops today do not have the privilege of living almost daily in the presence of the Savior, witnessing His miracles and learning directly from His lips as the apostles did.

Only God knows why the Holy Father has apparently not disciplined those of the hierarchy that have contributed negatively to the Church. This intelligent Pope is not easily misled. He has his reasons for his actions and we are to trust in the guidance of the Holy Spirit in the life of the Holy Father. Catholic newspapers are full of references to certain bishops who are suspected of no longer being really Catholic but are suspected of deliberately undermining the Church in apparent controversial decisions that seem to fly in the face of the Vatican and Catholic traditions. We are not wearing the "moccasins" of the Holy Father. We don't know what he knows at the highest level of the Church AND WE ARE NOT EXPECTED TO KNOW. We are expected to pray for the Pope and the bishops and we should be able to understand why IF we believe in the concept of spiritual warfare, which is more real than the car you drive or the chair you sit in.

God's ways are not our ways and He has his reasons for permitting the turmoil and dissensions within the Church. Our failure to live our Faith properly no doubt contributes to these conditions and God has chosen not to interfere with our decisions. The prime weapons in this time of spiritual warfare are prayer and fasting, based on a truly humble approach in our everyday actions, and the prudent way we approach all inquiries into apparent violations of Canon Law and the rubrics.

If we are to be members of that chosen few, the Remnant, we can expect that we will be put to the test, and possibly for the rest of our lifetime. As St. Paul said, we will someday reap the glory for the suffering we accept in our lifetime. Be consoled because the loyal Catholic is the instrument by which the true Catholic Faith will be preserved on earth. And in answer to Jesus' question— "When I return, will I find any Faith on earth?"- you will be able to kneel before Him and give a resounding "Yes."